Mistletoe
in Montana

by Pamela M. Kelley

Edited by Cindy Tahse
Cover by Susan Coils

ISBN: 978-1502381446

Also by Pamela M. Kelley

In loving memory of my mother, Marcia Claughton and my grandfather, Kenneth Ford.

Chapter One

Breaking up with someone was never an easy thing to do, and Traci Jones had been dreading this date all week. She and Billy Sears had briefly dated in high school and then started up again a few years ago. They'd been engaged for almost a year and Billy had been pushing recently to set a date and was growing ever more frustrated when Traci kept changing the subject. The time was long overdue to end things and she knew it wasn't going to be easy. But, it was necessary. Looking back, she could see that the signs were there, indicating trouble ahead, but she'd been oblivious to them, at first.

She had been caught up in Billy's easy charm and sunny good looks, his thick blonde hair, blue eyes and muscular build. He kept himself in very good shape and loved all the attention that he received. Billy had been a star quarterback in high school when Traci was a cheerleader, and he still spent most of his time at the high school even now in his role as gym teacher and football coach. Billy was the guy who was always the center of attention at parties, amusing at first, but after a few drinks he often grew loud and annoying.

Once they got engaged, Traci saw the troubling side of his personality more and more and started having doubts. It didn't help matters that Billy had a lingering back injury that flared up often. This meant he often took strong pain meds that seemed to make his mood swings even more dramatic.

It was her suggestion that they meet for an early dinner as Billy was too busy to do lunch. She'd suggested a more casual place, not wanting to give him the idea that this would be a romantic dinner, but Billy vetoed that and insisted on their favorite restaurant, Delancey's.

Fortunately, they had a corner booth in the back and it was just a few minutes past five; early still for the dinner rush so the restaurant was mostly empty. Which was good, in case Billy caused a scene.

Their waitress returned to the table with a glass of Shiraz for Traci and a Budweiser beer on draft for Billy. She took their orders and as soon as she walked away, Billy started in on her.

"What's going on with you and Christian Ford? Someone saw your car out at the ranch again. Do you think I'm stupid?"

Traci sighed. He was in a mood, which meant this was going to be even harder to do, and all the more necessary. These paranoid accusations by Billy were becoming a regular thing, and truth be told were starting to scare her a little. She wasn't stupid by any means, and could see the direction her life would go if she stayed with Billy, and she wanted no part of it. He hadn't gotten physically violent yet, but she could sense the potential simmering under the surface as his temper showed itself more frequently. For months now, his jealousy had been a problem as he was constantly texting her to see what she was doing and who she was with, and if he didn't like her answer, it was a problem.

"Yes, I was out at Christian Ford's ranch, again. You know I've been working with his wife, Molly, to redesign the Rose Cottage."

The waitress returned with their salads and a loaf of bread and Billy said nothing in response, just stabbed his fork into his salad and took a huge bite, glaring at Traci the whole time. She glanced at her watch, wondering how much longer it would be for their meals to arrive. She had no appetite at all, and just couldn't wait to get the break-up over with and go home. But, she didn't want to raise the subject until it was almost time to leave. She knew Billy too well, and knew it could get ugly fast.

"You got somewhere you need to be?" Billy asked. He'd seen her glance at her watch and was immediately suspicious, which was ridiculous. She'd never given him any reason to doubt her. She'd asked her twin brother, Travis, who was an attorney, for his advice recently, though she'd known what he was going to say. Travis hadn't been a fan of Billy's even from the beginning.

"He's not good enough for you," he had said simply. She'd wanted to try and understand where Billy's jealousy was coming from because it was a mystery to her.

"It's an insecurity thing, I'd bet. He's afraid of losing you, so he's trying to control you." He looked more serious as he continued, "I'm glad you're thinking of ending it. Frankly, from what you've told me lately, I'm afraid his behavior will escalate and you don't need that."

No, she didn't need that. Traci's life was going great, otherwise. She was 32 years old and owned her own small condo and her design business was growing steadily. Not enough for her to do it full-time, but she was getting there. She also worked part-time at Beauville's only department store. Snow's was a family run business and she enjoyed working there; plus, the discount was helpful as she was able to purchase many items for her decorating jobs- cute pillows, lamps, etc. At first, she'd thought Billy was the missing piece and had once imagined a life with him. He could be a lot of fun and he was great with kids. But the Billy she was dating now wasn't the same person. Maybe this was just a rough patch or maybe this was who he really was. Either way, Traci was no longer interested in sticking around to find out.

Their dinners arrived and Traci tried to make small talk while they ate and focused the conversation on happier things, like the high school football team's recent win. That put Billy in a better mood, and once the waitress cleared their plates and brought them each a cup of coffee, Traci cleared her throat. It was time.

"Billy, we need to talk," she said gently.

"We do?" He was busy pouring sugar into his coffee and didn't seem to be paying much attention.

"I think you're really great, and I've enjoyed our time together, but I've been thinking a lot lately and I'm not ready to get married, not to you, not to anyone. So, I think it's probably for the best that we end things, so we can both move on." She wiggled her diamond engagement ring off her finger and set it down on the table between them. That got his attention.

"What are you talking about?" Billy wasn't mad yet, just seriously confused and Traci felt awful as she watched him try to process what had just happened. "You're breaking up with me?"

"I'm really sorry, but I think it's for the best."

"The best for who? Who are you seeing, then? There has to be someone else."

"There's no one else," she assured him. "It's not about another guy. It's just about me and what I want."

"And you don't want me anymore." He was angry now and Traci couldn't really blame him. He hadn't seen this coming.

"I really think it's for the best," she repeated.

"You don't mean it. We can work this out. Let's just take a break, some time apart. Then see how it goes?" His tone had shifted from angry to pleading to oddly calm and determined. He smiled at the waitress as she dropped off the check. "I got this."

"I don't want to take a break," Traci said. But Billy didn't seem to be listening.

"We'll touch base in a few weeks. I'll call you." Traci took a final sip of her coffee and then stood up. This hadn't gone down quite the way she'd expected. She'd anticipated more of a melt-down of sorts, but also an ending, not a 'to-be-continued.' She really didn't want to have this conversation again.

Chapter Two

*D*aniel Ford leaned forward to get a better look at one of his target stocks. He had three monitors across his desktop, all split into index-card sized stock charts lit in various colors and moving in real time, up or down along with the market. His target stock for the day was doing exactly what his research had predicted. Two more ticks up and then he clicked into his trading account and quickly entered a sell order. Less than a minute later it was executed and Dan was many thousands of dollars richer. It was a good day.

He was ready to wrap things up and was planning to meet a few of his friends after work at their usual Thursday night spot, Richie's Pub, which was just a few miles down the road. First, though, he had to do his daily blog and video posts for his readers.

He quickly created his blog post for the day, along with a

quick two minute video discussing why the trades he'd made that day had worked, or not, and what he was looking for in the coming days. As always, he explained that he had stop losses set as well as sell orders in place once certain target prices were hit. That way, he was protected if the market moved quickly in either direction and for some reason he wasn't able to act. Some people thought he was overly cautious to do that, but Dan took a very conservative approach to trading. This, as it turned out, would be a very good thing.

As soon as he finished up for the day, he jumped in the shower, then changed and went to meet the guys for drinks. Because he worked from home and was by himself all day, Dan was usually feeling a bit stir-crazy once five o'clock rolled around. To get his people-fix, he went out almost every night. Living in Chicago, there was always something to do and people to do it with, even if it was just meeting the guys for a few drinks after work. That was actually his favorite thing to do, catching up with his closest friends at the local pub. Dan drove a Jeep Cherokee and had a reserved spot in front of his building.

There was no traffic, and he was just a block from Richie's Pub when a Ford Explorer came flying around the corner and he didn't have time to react. The other car took the turn too widely and plowed right into him.

The next thing he knew, he was in a strange room feeling groggy and staring into the eyes of his older brother, which was really strange because Christian lived thousands of miles away, in Montana.

The doctor said he was lucky. No internal damage, just a broken leg. But it was broken in three places and would take months to heal correctly. He'd be on crutches for at least two months, probably longer. He was half-asleep as his brother and doctor discussed his treatment plan and when Christian suggested that he recuperate in Montana, he murmured in agreement before falling fast asleep again.

Christian stayed at Dan's place that night and packed a suitcase full of clothes as well as his two laptops. They left the next day to fly back to Beauville, Montana, where Christian lived and where Dan had grown up. Dan didn't love the idea of spending that much time away from Chicago, but he didn't have a good second option. His condo was on the fourth floor of a beautiful old building that was a walkup, meaning no elevator. His other friends that lived nearby were in similar situations. There was no way he could deal with four flights of stairs.

❧

It was strange being back in Beauville. Christian brought his bags in for him and set them in his grandfather's old room, just outside the kitchen. It was a great room, but his grandfather hadn't been gone long. Dan had come home for the funeral a few months back and other than that, he generally only visited Beauville once a year, at Thanksgiving, because he wouldn't see his brother or grandfather if he didn't make the trip. Dan had made his feelings about Beauville clear many years ago. It was a small town and not enough going on to keep him interested in sticking around.

It was different for his brother, Christian. He loved the ranch, and loved building things. He was able to do a combination of both by taking over their grandfather's business and expanding it into real estate development after he'd graduated from college with a dual degree in architecture and business.

Dan escaped from Beauville by attending college in Chicago, and once he had had a taste of city life, he'd realized that he never wanted to live in Beauville again. Chicago, with its fast pace and everything it had to offer, felt like home. Spending the next few months in Beauville was a curveball that didn't excite him in the least. He just hoped the internet connection was strong enough that he'd be able to work. Christian promised that it was, but Dan was doubtful.

Fortunately, Christian was correct and the wifi connection was excellent. Dan was able to spread his collection of laptops across the kitchen table and simulate his workstation of electronic stock-charts. Once he was all plugged in, he was back in business. He'd only lost a day of work, as the accident had happened on a Thursday night. Because he was so conservative with stop-loss targets on everything, his portfolio had automatically executed on several trades and while he hadn't made a ton of money, he didn't have any large losses, either.

Chapter Three

A month later, Dan had settled in well enough, but still often felt like a third wheel in his brother's house. Christian's wife, Molly, was as nice as could be, but he couldn't help feeling like he was cramping their style as they were newlyweds. His brother had tried to brush his worries away.

"Don't be ridiculous. You know the deal with Molly. We're just friends, and once we hit the six month mark, we're free to go our separate ways and she'll be heading back to Manhattan."

Dan wasn't so sure about that. Their grandfather had left most of the ranch to Christian as he was the one running it and had expanded it over the years to include the real estate development side of the business; but Gramps had also wanted him to settle down, to get married and start a family. He knew that without a push, that wasn't likely to happen, so he added a condition into the will. Christian had to marry the girl Gramps had picked out, Molly Bishop, and they had to stay married for six months. Then, if they chose, they could end the marriage.

Molly was once their neighbor when she was a child and Gramps had run into her a month or so before he died and had changed his will immediately after. Molly's mother and aunt lived in Beauville and she'd been home for a brief visit. Dan had thought the idea was crazy at first and had been thankful that Gramps hadn't left any such conditions for him; but now that he'd spent some time with Molly, he wondered if his grandfather might have been sharper than they gave him credit for. There was definitely something brewing between Molly and Christian and Dan fully approved, but also worried that his sudden appearance might have slowed down that momentum. He was deep in thought when Mrs. O'Brien, who had been the family's housekeeper for over twenty years, pulled up a chair at the kitchen table that he used as his office during the day.

"Am I interrupting anything?" she asked, as she added cream to her mug of coffee.

"No, not at all. The stocks are not doing much at the moment." Dan's many colored stock charts were blinking but not moving really in either direction. The market seemed to be taking a break. It was a good time for him to do the same.

"Those screens look like a bunch of gibberish to me. Reminds me of a pilot dashboard or air traffic control."

He chuckled. "That's actually a good analogy. All of these charts let me track multiple stocks at the same time and to see immediately when one starts to move up or down."

Mrs. O'Brien sipped her coffee. She'd tip-toed around him during his first month, and he knew that she worried that she'd be interrupting his intense focus. Every now and then, she'd drop a chocolate banana shake or sandwich off for him, setting it carefully by his computer, and then she'd be on her way back to dusting or cleaning or whatever project she was working on. Dan liked having her around fussing over him; it was a nice change from the cold emptiness of his apartment. But, he knew he couldn't get too used to it; in two months, he'd be cleared to drive and to fly back home to Chicago.

"How'd you end up doing this kind of work? I thought you went off to be a journalist?" Mrs. O'Brien asked.

"I started out as a journalist. During school I worked part-time at the Chicago Tribune, and then after graduating they offered me a full-time role." He'd been lucky to get it, too; it was rare for a fresh grad to land a permanent role at the paper. He'd managed it because they knew his work by then.

"They put me on the financial beat. Chicago is the home of the options exchange and I spent a lot of time learning the ins and outs, discovered I had a knack for it. Dabbled a little here and there and started a blog to document my experiments. Next thing I knew, my trades worked more often than they didn't and people started paying attention to what I was doing and what I was saying. And here I am."

The blog quickly developed a rabid following and when someone suggested that he charge for the information he was sharing freely, he thought they were crazy, that no one would be interested. But they were. The revenue from his monthly private blog subscriptions tripled his salary at the paper by the end of the year and the money he made from the actual trades was insane. Still, it wasn't easy to leave the paper; he loved being a journalist and didn't want to give it up completely. Fortunately, he didn't have to.

"Luckily, the paper still wanted me to do the occasional story for them, and a few other magazines, too. Bigger more in-depth pieces which also helps to promote the blog, so it's worked out well."

"Your parents would be so proud of you," Mrs. O'Brien said and then added, "Of both you boys."

They were quiet for a moment then. Mrs. O'Brien finished her coffee and Dan thought about his parents. They'd been gone for over ten years now, killed by a drunk driver on Christmas Eve, but he still missed them terribly, especially around the holidays. He wasn't a big fan of the Christmas season; it held nothing but bad memories for him. Every year he dreaded the month of December and breathed a sigh of relief in January. He was on track to be home by the beginning of December, which was a good thing. In Chicago, he could withdraw and be a hermit for a few weeks and no one would be the wiser, especially given his job where he worked alone at home. He'd never get away with that here. His brother loved the holiday season and he suspected this small town also embraced it. He would be hit in the face with holiday cheer everywhere. Good thing he was going to be long gone by then.

"Have you seen Traci yet?" Mrs. O'Brien was talking and Dan snapped back to attention. Traci, who was Traci? Then it came to him; she was Travis Jones's twin sister. Travis was his brother's best friend and Molly talked constantly about the great job Traci was doing helping to decorate the Rose Cottage.

"I haven't seen many people yet. Just Molly's mother and her Aunt Betty, they stopped by a few days ago. Hopefully, I'll get out soon. I'm just about at the point where the doctor said I could put some weight on my foot. Truthfully, I'm getting a little stir crazy." He grinned at Mrs. O'Brien and she gave his arm a pat.

"I've heard stories about you," she said. "That you like to flirt with all the girls, but never get serious about any of them. You're what, 34 now, right? Maybe you should stay here instead of going back to Chicago. Find a nice girl, and settle down. Your brother would love that. We all would. It's nice to be near family."

Dan had zero interest in settling down any time soon, and even less interest in staying in Beauville any longer than he had to, so he avoided the subject by asking, "So, what's up with Traci?"

Mrs. O'Brien leaned forward, with a gleam in her eye. "She's single now, just dumped that fellow she was engaged to."

It had been so long since he'd lived here that he felt like he barely knew anyone. He'd seen Travis a few times over the years as he and Christian were best friends, but it had been much longer since he'd seen Traci. From what he remembered, she'd always been a bit of a tomboy, short hair, into sports and even building things. She and Travis had worked part-time during the summer for Gramps, doing light construction. Last time he had seen Traci she was wearing overalls and swinging a hammer. Not exactly his type.

Though truthfully, Dan didn't really have a type. He loved women and dated a lot. He was popular in Chicago and moved in a hot crowd that was seen at all the right places. His friends were also successful in the financial world. They ran hedge funds, managed money, and didn't hesitate to spend it. Women were attracted to that and Dan enjoyed getting out and about. Because he was home alone every day, intensely focused on watching his computer screens and not missing anything, he was ready to get out most nights. That's another thing he missed about being here. He hadn't gotten out at all.

"Well, we should both probably get back to work." Mrs. O'Brien stood up and glanced at his computer screens. "Looks like something is starting to happen."

Dan brought his attention back to the screens and leaned forward. Something was definitely happening. Must have been some kind of announcement because all of the stocks were starting to climb, and a few began to drop steadily. Time to focus.

Traci enjoyed working at Snow's. It was a family run general store, and carried everything from furniture to kitchen and bath items, books, even an appliance and hardware section. Traci was usually in the home goods area, which suited her fine. Working at Snow's helped with her design business as well, as she not only got a nice discount on everything, but she also had a pulse on what was moving in the market, what items and trends seemed to be most popular. Plus, she enjoyed interacting with people, especially as she knew a majority of the customers.

Her shift ended at five and business had been steady most of the day. At a quarter to five, she had a small line of customers waiting to be rung up when out of the corner of her eye she caught a glimpse of someone familiar heading her way. It was Billy. He was smiling as he walked towards her and was holding something bulky wrapped in paper. As he got closer, she saw it was a bouquet of flowers, and her stomach clenched. She hadn't seen Billy in several weeks and was starting to relax. Now this. He stood at the end of the line and waited his turn. Traci's only relief was that there was no one else behind him. No one to witness the scene that she knew was coming.

She finished ringing up the last customer and then faced Billy. He spoke first.

"Hi, Traci. You look beautiful. As always."

"Um, thank you." She glanced around nervously, but still no one else was in the immediate area. Thank goodness.

"I brought these for you. I've missed you so much. Your shift ends in a few minutes, right?" Traci had a set schedule, which Billy knew. The thought made her uneasy, to think that he was keeping track of her. "I thought we could go have a nice dinner, catch up, and maybe start over." He was laying on the charm, but it was too much. His cutesy confidence, which she used to find endearing, now just annoyed her. She didn't like to be pushed and Billy was pushing. Why couldn't he just accept that things were over?

"Billy, I meant what I said. I don't want to go to dinner. I'm sorry."

A muscle flickered in Billy's jaw as he clenched his teeth. In a swift move that surprised her, he grabbed the bouquet of red roses with both hands, snapped them in half and threw them in the trash can next to the register.

"You can't just toss me aside like that. I'm not finished with you, with us yet. I'll check back with you in a few weeks." His mood had shifted so quickly from charm to intense anger that Traci, without even realizing it, had taken a step backwards.

"Billy, I think you should leave." Traci glanced around the store and was both relieved and concerned to see several people heading her way. Tom, the store manager, was in his early sixties and was like a father figure to Traci. He'd obviously picked up on the tense vibe.

"Everything all right over here?" He glanced at Billy and then back at Traci.

"I was just leaving," Billy said, his voice a bit calmer now, which was no less disturbing to Traci as she watched him walk away.

❧

Traci stopped by her mother's house on the way home from work. She was glad to see her brother Travis's car in the driveway, too. They laughed about it, but there really was some kind of twin radar. Too many times to count, they often showed up at the same place within minutes of each other or one would call their mother and seconds later the other would beep in. So, it didn't surprise her that he was here. They both often dropped by for quick visits after work.

Travis was sitting at the kitchen table opening a beer as their mother scurried around looking for her favorite necklace that she was sure she'd left somewhere in the kitchen.

"Ah ha!" She spotted it next to the toaster and pounced.

"Hi, honey," she called out as Traci set her bag down and pulled out a chair next to Travis.

"Where are you off to?" she asked her mom.

"Your father and I are going to dinner at the Anderson's. He should be home any minute and then we're heading out. I'm so glad you both stopped by, though. Help me close this clasp, would you?" Traci stood up and snapped the tiny closure of the necklace for her mother.

"Thank you, now I can relax. Join me for a small glass of wine?"

"Sure." Traci was ready for a glass. It had been a long day. The department store was busier than usual and she'd been startled by the surprise visit from Billy. It had been a few weeks since she'd last seen him at Delancey's. At first she'd thought he was going to make things difficult, that it hadn't sunken in that she really wanted to end things and she had been on edge the first week or two. But when she hadn't heard a peep from Billy, she had finally started to relax. And then he showed up at the store. It had completely unsettled her and she needed to talk about it.

Her mother set two glasses of red wine on the table, then pulled out a chair and sat down. Traci picked up a glass and took a sip.

"Billy came to see me today."

That got their attention. "What?" and "Where?" both Travis and her mother spoke at once and both looked concerned. She filled them in on Billy's visit.

"He came by the store. I had a line of people waiting to check out and he just stood there, smiling, until they were all gone. Then he handed me a bouquet of flowers, told me how much he loved me and missed me and asked me out to dinner."

"You didn't fall for that I hope?" Travis's eyes flashed anger that she knew was directed at Billy. Her mother looked nervous.

"Of course not. I told him it was over, again, and that we both needed to move on. I don't think he's ready to do that, though. He said he'd check back with me in a few weeks." She didn't tell them that he'd first snapped the bouquet in half and thrown it in the trash before taking a deep breath and forcing a smile. To say he made her nervous was an understatement.

"Maybe you should get a restraining order," Travis suggested.

Traci had considered that but at this point didn't want to further aggravate Billy. She was still hopeful that it would sink in soon and he'd just move on to someone else.

"I'll think about that," she said.

"What are your plans for dinner?" Travis asked. Traci had no plans other than heading home, putting on a pair of comfy sweats and maybe heating up some soup. Nothing too exciting.

"Nothing. What did you have in mind?"

"I'm dying for a good steak. Want to join me for a bite to eat at Delancey's? My treat."

Traci smiled. "How can I say no to that?" She was still feeling more than a bit unsettled after the confrontation with Billy and a nice dinner with her brother would help to get her mind off things.

"Here's your father now," their mother said as a car pulled into the driveway. "Have fun, you two."

Chapter Four

Molly walked in the door a few minutes past five, just as Dan was finishing up his blog and video posts for the day. Dan really liked Molly and thought she was great for his brother. He'd noticed that Christian seemed to have loosened up a bit and smiled more than he'd ever seen in the past. Molly was easy to be around. She was warm and friendly and full of energy.

"How's it going over there?" he asked. If Molly stayed married to Christian for at least six months, according to the terms of their grandfather's will, the Rose Cottage, which was about a half a mile down the road, and was the house his grandparents had lived in, would be hers. Christian had suggested that a minor remodel and some decorating could turn the place into a sweet Bed & Breakfast. And it would give Molly something to focus on during her time in Beauville. Christian had also filled him in that she was up for a promotion to general manager at the fancy hotel she worked at in Manhattan and that he hoped that coming out here wouldn't slow that down too much.

"It's going really well so far. Traci did such an amazing job with the decorating and the opening weekend was a success. We've been busier each week." Dan knew that Traci had done the decorating at his brother's place, too, so imagined that the Rose Cottage looked impressive.

"That's great," he said. Then, as he saw Molly staring at his chocolate shake, he added, "I need to lay off these. I've gained seven or eight pounds since I've been here."

Molly chuckled. "It's probably from being less active, too. I wouldn't worry much about it."

"True. I feel like a little old man right now, stiff from sitting all day." He eased himself up from the chair and onto his crutches and did a few laps around the kitchen. "Feels good to stretch."

"Did Mrs. O'Brien leave dinner for us?" Molly said as she glanced around the kitchen.

"She made a bunch of stuffed shells earlier and put them in the fridge. Said we can heat them up whenever."

"Okay, I can make us a salad and I think we have bread still."

"Do you think Christian might be up for going out for a change?" Dan said. "I'm feeling a little stir crazy."

Molly looked surprised and a bit hesitant. "Sure, if you think you're up for it." Dan hadn't left the house once since he'd arrived; he was more than up for it. He needed to get out.

"I think it would be okay now. It will be four weeks tomorrow."

They walked into Delancey's forty-five minutes later. Dan was able to move pretty quickly on his crutches and he'd also changed while Christian was in the shower. He'd put on jeans and a hunter green button down shirt that he'd been told highlighted his green eyes and dark blonde hair. He'd even shaved. He was pleased to notice out of the corner of his eye that even though he was on crutches, more than one female guest took a long look as he walked by.

They were seated quickly at a great table near where the band would soon be setting up. Dan was surprised when he saw there was going to be entertainment.

"Impressive. Didn't know you had any places like this in Beauville."

"A lot has changed since you lived here," Christian began. "The town has grown, is still growing."

"So, what's good here?" Dan asked, as the waitress handed them menus. He smiled at her and she immediately seemed flustered.

"Everything's good, everything. Can I get you something to drink?" She took their drink orders and then scurried off.

"I know you're getting back to normal now. The ladies here don't stand a chance," Christian said with a chuckle.

"The steak is what's really good here," Molly told him as the waitress returned with their drinks and Dan told her they needed a little more time to decide.

"Okay, steak it is then." As he closed his menu, he noticed

Travis and a woman that he didn't recognize walk in. Christian saw them, too, and waved them over.

"Are you guys here for dinner? Join us, we just ordered drinks."

"Great, I just had a crazy day and told Traci I'd buy her dinner if she agreed to come out." Ah, so that was Traci. He never would have recognized her. The tomboy was gone. This Traci had long, dark brown hair that fell in soft, shiny waves. It was beautiful. She was beautiful. Her eyes were a dark, deep blue that stood out against her dark hair and fair skin. She was tall, maybe 5' 8", but so was he at 6' 2". He caught her gaze and felt something unfamiliar and powerful. He was suddenly very glad that he'd insisted on getting out for the night.

"He didn't have to twist my arm too hard," Traci laughed.

The waitress returned just then and pulled a chair over to their table so there was room for all of them, and both Travis and Traci sat down.

"Dan, you remember Traci?" Travis said as he picked up a menu.

"Of course, though it has been a while," he said.

Once they all had their drinks and had put their dinner orders in, Christian proposed a toast:

"To Dan's first night out in Beauville."

"And to many more," Travis added.

They all clicked glasses and the conversation flowed easily as they ate their salads.

Until Traci asked Molly, "Have you heard about Isabella's opening special?" Isabella Graham was Christian's ex-girlfriend. According to Christian, they were never serious, but she wasn't happy to be dumped out of left field because Christian was about to marry someone else. To his credit, Dan knew that Christian had given her the full explanation of their grandfather's will, but still, she was a bit put out. So much so, that she'd recently announced that she was also going to be opening a bed and breakfast in town. Supposedly, it was her great-uncle's idea as he had a huge old Victorian that was sitting empty. Isabella had no hotel or restaurant experience but had told Christian she wasn't worried about it as it looked easy enough.

"We've already had two cancellations because of it. I don't blame them, really. It's a good deal."

"What is she doing?" Christian looked at Molly in surprise. She usually kept him posted on everything.

"I just saw the ad in today's paper. She's running an opening day special, two nights for the price of one, including weekends."

"Can she do that?" Christian addressed the question to Travis.

Travis hesitated for a moment, then said, "As Isabella's attorney, I shouldn't be discussing this with you, but yeah, it's totally legal."

"Just because it's legal, doesn't make it right." Traci glared at her brother, who looked decidedly uncomfortable at the direction the conversation had taken.

"It's all right," Molly assured all of them. "It's inconvenient for us, but I don't blame her for doing it. It's a business decision, something any competitor would do."

"You wouldn't do it," Traci said loyally.

"No, I would if it made sense to do it. It wouldn't have been my strategy for a grand opening, though."

This caught Dan's attention, "Why not? Seems like a good idea to me."

"I'm just more cautious," Molly explained. "I'm a bit of a worrier, though. We had a slow opening, just two rooms rented and that was perfect for me. I wanted to make sure everything went smoothly."

"And it did," Christian said proudly and Molly smiled back at him.

"Slow has never been Isabella's speed," Travis said as he reached for another roll.

"I don't suppose you got an invite to her opening party?" Traci directed the question at Molly.

"No, when is it?"

"This Thursday, the night before she officially opens. Isn't that exactly what you did?"

Molly just nodded and then asked, "Are you going?"

"I haven't decided yet. I don't have anyone to go with now. Travis will already be there. They have an appointment just before the party begins."

"I'll go with you," Dan surprised himself by saying. "I'm getting really stir crazy and that will get me out of the house. And I can be the lone family representative or spy, however you want to look at it."

"Are you sure?" Traci's attention was on him now and Dan felt strangely nervous, hoping she'd agree and wondering where his usual confidence had disappeared to.

"Yeah, it'll be fun," he said as he noticed the others looking at him with interest. Christian was frowning and Dan knew he'd have something to say about this when they got home.

"Oh, good. I'll swing by to pick you up around six then, if that works for you," Tracie said.

"I'll be ready."

* * *

"What are you doing with Traci?" Christian started in on him on the ride home.

"Just helping out. She needed someone to go to the party with and I'm available."

"Don't pull your usual behavior with her. Traci's not like the other girls you date."

"You don't know any of the girls I've dated."

"You know what I mean. I know enough from what you've told me over the years. Traci's a nice girl, and she's going through a rough time right now."

"What's wrong?"

"She finally went through with dumping her fiance," Molly explained. "He was getting too controlling, violent even. It scared her."

"He hit her?" Good thing she'd dumped the guy.

"No. It never got to that point. Not yet. But Traci was feeling uneasy that it could be heading in that direction. Billy has some issues with chronic pain and is on some serious meds at times. It's made him moody and unpredictable."

"She did the right thing, then."

"So, don't mess with her," Christian warned.

"I'll be on my best behavior," Dan said, looking to lighten the mood.

"Yeah, that's what worries me," Christian said with a chuckle.

Traci debated what to wear to Isabella's opening. She generally hated networking events like this, but she knew it was important to get out there and talk to people as it did sometimes result in landing a design project and she need-ed all the work she could get. She pulled two dresses out of her closet and held them up. The black one was a safe, pro-fessional choice. She could blend into the crowd well. It was dark and somber and fit her mood perfectly. The red one was festive and merry. It was made out of a soft cashmere blend and the simple V-neck and vibrant color was flattering against her dark hair. She hadn't worn the red one in over a year and slipped it on to see how it looked.

It still fit perfectly and she immediately felt her mood lift. The rosy red brought out the color in her cheeks and made her feel happy. With that question settled, Traci finished get-ting ready and then headed out to the ranch to pick up Dan. He was ready to go when she arrived and although he was still using crutches, he moved quickly on them. They settled into Traci's car and chatted easily during the ten minute drive to Isabella's party.

A valet was waiting as they drove into the circular drive-way. Traci handed him the keys and waited as Dan got out of the car and onto his crutches. There was a small crowd milling about outside admiring the landscaping and working water fountains by the entrance. They made their way inside, found a small cocktail table to settle at, and then Traci went to get them both a drink. It was an impressive crowd. All the important people in town were there.

Before she could even get to the bar, a handsome waiter stopped and offered to bring her a drink. Traci ordered a glass of pinot grigio for herself and a beer for Dan. Within minutes, the waiter was back with her drinks and she brought them back to the table where Dan was sitting and looking about the room.

"You'd never know I grew up in this town," he chuckled. "This just looks like a sea of strangers to me."

Traci settled into the other chair at the table and took a sip of her wine. She glanced around the room, which was getting packed. "She has quite a turnout for this. Seems like a bigger crowd than Molly had even, though I see most of the same faces."

"People are curious, probably wondering about a rivalry, I suppose," Dan said. He then added, "Plus, there's really not much else going on in this town."

"It's not that bad," Traci laughed.

"No, you're right. It's actually much different than I remember. The town has grown, and changed a lot since I last lived here."

"What do you like so much about Chicago?" Traci had never been there, and it sounded very far away and exciting.

Dan took a sip of his beer, leaned back and smiled.

"What's not to love? Chicago's fantastic. I fell in love with the city when I went to school there. There's so much history, and culture. Tons of restaurants; Chicago is known for great food. And there are plenty of opportunities for work, especially in the financial markets; that's the area I focus in."

"It sounds wonderful. I bet you're missing it."

"I am, but it's also kind of nice taking a break, no pun intended. I haven't spent any real time here since before college. It's been fun and relaxing catching up with Christian and Mrs. O'Brien."

"You like how she spoils you. I've heard about those shakes."

Dan smiled and Traci thought the laugh lines that appeared around his mouth and eyes only made him look that much cuter. Too bad he would be going home soon. He was fun to be around and very easy on the eyes.

"So, which one is the infamous Isabella?" he asked.

Traci looked around trying to spot her. "There she is, coming towards us." Isabella radiated pure glamour, and Traci was impressed with her outfit. Isabella always looked amazing. She was one of those people who seemed to have a knack for making even basic blue jeans and a t-shirt look fashionable, and tonight she looked like she'd stepped out of the pages of a magazine. Her dark brown, almost black hair tumbled down her back in a cascade of perfect, loose curls and her dress was a deep, bottle-green crushed velvet that flattered her hour-glass figure. Her heels were high, as always, which let her hips sway just a bit as she walked. A long strand of creamy pearls completed the outfit and Traci almost giggled when she saw the look on Dan's face as she approached their table. He looked positively star-struck.

"Traci, so glad you could make it." Isabella greeted them warmly as she glanced at Dan and then held out her hand.

"You look familiar, but I don't think we've met? Isabella Graham."

Dan shook her hand and then said, "Dan Ford, Christian's brother."

"Of course, now I see the resemblance. Please tell Christian and Molly I said hello." She smiled sweetly then and swept away to greet another guest.

"So that's Isabella," Dan said. "She almost seems the complete opposite of Molly. Beautiful girl, though."

Traci thought of Molly and her casual, girl-next-door looks and easy-going ways and chuckled. "Yes, they are night and day." She watched Isabella chatting animatedly with an older gentleman who seemed to be hanging on her every word. Isabella was dramatic and charismatic, outgoing and always the center of attention, as people were drawn to her. Real estate sales was the perfect career for her. Running an inn, well, that remained to be seen.

From what Traci could see, Isabella had done a nice job of decorating, though. The main lobby, where they were sitting, was warm and inviting, the walls painted a soft moss green, accented with rich cream trim and deep burgundy window treatments. The floors were hard wood, topped with coordinating oriental rugs that added warmth to the room. Off to the side, a large fireplace cast a soft glow. Handsome young men wearing black and white circled the room, passing out appetizers. Traci felt her stomach rumble a bit and realized she hadn't eaten anything yet. So, when a server approached them, she eagerly accepted a piece of steak on a stick.

"This is Wagyu beef...be sure to compare with what Rodney is passing out, the grass-fed," the server said. "Isabella wants everyone to know that she'll be having occasional wine dinners that will include both, to highlight local vendors and the highest quality meat available."

"Poor guy has to say that spiel to everyone," Dan said as he took a bite of steak, and then added, "Wow, this is good stuff."

"They don't have steak in Chicago?" Traci teased.

"Not like this." He nodded at the next waiter who approached their table, offering the grass-fed beef. They both took a small skewer and then Traci asked, "Which one do you like better?"

"They're both good. Too close to call."

Over the next hour, they enjoyed a second drink and an array of appetizers from bite-sized spinach pies, to stuffed mushrooms, mini-crabcakes and small plastic martini glasses filled with cocktail sauce and plump, juicy shrimp. Dan was fun and easy to talk to and Traci was glad he'd offered to come with her. It took her mind off worrying about Billy.

Her brother, Travis, joined them after making the rounds and saying hello to everyone he knew, which was the majority of the people there. As a general lawyer, Travis handled all aspects of law, lots of real estate and anything else that came up. He was one of just a few lawyers in town and had built a steady practice over the years. He and Dan were mid-conversation when Travis frowned and stopped talking.

"Billy's here and just spotted you. He's coming this way." Traci took a sip of wine to calm her nerves which were immediately on edge as Billy caught her eye and picked up his pace. His face was stormy and Traci braced herself for a scene. Hopefully, having Travis by her side would be a deterrent.

"Who's this?" Billy asked as he arrived at their table. Traci was about to introduce Dan when Travis jumped in instead, and Traci breathed a sigh of relief. She knew that Travis was trying to give the impression that Dan was there with him, not on any kind of a date with Traci. It really wasn't anyway, but she knew Billy would assume otherwise.

"Dan, meet Billy. Billy this is Christian's brother, Dan, visiting for a bit from Chicago." Billy looked suspiciously around the table.

"Nice to meet you," he said finally. "How long are you here for?"

"A few months; as soon as this leg heals up, I'll be on my way back to Chicago." Billy seemed to relax a bit at that and his tone of voice changed.

"How are you, Traci? You look beautiful, as always."

"Thanks, I'm good Billy. I think we were just about to head out. It was nice seeing you," she said politely.

"Right, I'll see you around, then. Nice to meet you," Billy said to Dan and then watched from a distance as the three of them made their way out.

"Wow, that's your ex? He's intense," Dan said as they drove away.

"Yeah, he can be. Luckily Travis was sitting with us. There would have been more of a scene if it had just been the two of us."

A few minutes later, Traci pulled into the ranch driveway and hopped out to get Dan's crutches out of the backseat and then walked with him to the front door. He gave her a look of appreciation as she opened the door for him.

"Thanks. It was good to get out and about."

"I'm glad you were able to make it."

"Maybe we can hang out again sometime before I have to leave?"

"I'd like that." Traci smiled. Dan would be the perfect person to spend time with right now. He was just here for a short time, so there was no pressure or expectations, just someone fun to be around. That was about all she could handle at the moment. The idea of jumping into a relationship, with anyone, was something she wasn't ready for. Especially with the holidays around the corner. Christmas was her favorite time of year, and she was looking forward to keeping busy, and enjoying it with family and friends.

Chapter Five

The next month went by quickly, considering how anxious Dan was to get back to Chicago. He kept busy with work and the physical therapy exercises he'd been instructed to do on his own, mostly stretching and some light weights to keep the muscles strong. He still needed to use the crutches to get around, but his leg didn't ache as much as it used to, so that was good. He'd gone out a few times over the past few weeks, with Molly, Christian and Travis usually. He hadn't called Traci directly to ask her to come with them, but had suggested that Christian tell Travis to bring her along. Christian had shot him a warning look each time and then came back to say that Traci was working the night shift once and out with friends another time. He gave up after that. It was obvious Christian didn't approve, even though he was simply looking for someone to do things with, and to be fair,

didn't want to give the wrong impression to Traci, either. Only one month to go, and then he'd be home and back in his usual routine. His friends had kept in touch often at first, emails and texts about all the fun things they were doing. But, as the weeks went by, the communications slowed and he couldn't blame them. They were busy and he was far away.

He found himself in a bit of a mood, feeling somewhat sorry for himself, and more than anything he was bored silly and feeling restless. It was a little past five and Molly wasn't home yet from the Inn. Mrs. O'Brien had left almost an hour ago and he had no idea where Christian was; he was usually home by now. Dan decided to take a walk outside, get some fresh air and a little exercise, and to just do a lap around the main yard on his crutches.

He grabbed his coat and his crutches and stepped outside. The cool air rushed over him and he zipped his down jacket up tight and started walking. Thanksgiving was just a few weeks away and it was starting to feel like winter already. The lights were on around the yard, but it was getting dark quickly and Dan began to rethink this idea. Maybe it would be best to go on this kind of a walk in broad daylight. He sighed and was about to head back in when he heard a scream coming from one of the stables and stopped in his tracks. He heard the sound again and realized it was just two of the stable hands goofing around. Satisfied that everything was fine, he started on his way again but his next step went very wrong. He thought he was stepping on hard earth, but because of the darkness, he missed seeing a small pothole that threw his balance off and he went down hard and felt a sharp ping.

The sudden pain took his breath away. He was stuck now; he couldn't lift himself back up without putting his weight on his leg and he knew he'd re-injured himself. He just didn't know how bad it was. He sat there on the cold ground, fuming. He didn't even have his cell phone on him to call anyone. He cursed his own stupidity. It was a very long ten minutes before he finally saw the lights of Christian's truck coming down the driveway. Christian pulled in and parked and the lights hit him head on, highlighting him in all his glory, sprawled awkwardly on the ground.

"What happened? Are you okay?" Christian called out as he walked over.

"I've fallen and I can't get up!" Dan tried to make a lame joke about the situation, but knew it wasn't funny.

Christian grabbed his crutches and then helped him up. He walked with him as he slowly made his way into the house with the use of the crutches.

Once inside, he collapsed on a chair in the kitchen and tried to catch his breath. He could feel beads of sweat along his forehead from the effort. His brother quickly sized up the situation.

"It's freezing out there, and you're sweating and can barely move. I think we need to get you to the ER, see how much damage you did."

Dan just nodded. What could he say? His brother was right.

❧

Four hours later, they met with the doctor, who by now had reviewed a new set of X-rays. They were in the local hospital, and had been waiting for what felt like years. Dan only had to have the leg X-rayed but there were other higher priority cases ahead of them, so they waited their turn, until finally Dan was brought in, examined, and the leg X-rayed.

"Well, you did a nice number on that leg. Wasn't enough that you broke it in three places already, huh?" Dr. Jarvis was a crusty, older doc, early sixties if Dan had to guess, and clearly thought he was a comedian. Dan just nodded.

"Well, the good news is that you didn't break it again. The bad news is that it looks like you shifted things around, maybe sprained something. Kind of sets the clock back on your recovery, I'd say."

"How long?" Dan asked.

"At least another month before you're ready to lose the crutches. You need to be careful and baby that leg. Take it slow for the next two weeks, then start back on your physical therapy. Don't walk in the dark," he scolded.

Dan was quiet on the way back to the ranch. He finally spoke as they were pulling into the driveway. He'd been thinking, a lot, for the past few hours.

"I'm sorry about this," he said to Christian.

"Don't apologize to me. It's your leg," his brother laughed. "I bet you're ready for a cold beer by now."

"Absolutely."

Molly was in the kitchen reading a magazine and eating a slice of pizza when they walked in. Christian had called her on the way to hospital, and they filled her in on Dan's injury while Christian opened two bottles of beer, an IPA from a local brewery.

"There's pizza in the oven, still warm, it was just delivered about ten minutes ago," Molly said as she grabbed another piece for herself. Christian got plates and took a few slices for him and Dan and then joined them at the kitchen table.

"So, I've been thinking," Dan began. "Since it looks like I'm going to be here for a bit longer than expected, I think I want to move into the guesthouse."

Christian frowned at that idea. "I know Gramps left you that piece of the property, but no one has even been in that house for over a year. It's got to be musty. There's no reason to do that."

"I thought I was only going to be here for one more month. Now it looks like two, maybe three. I can't keep camping out in your house. You guys need your privacy."

Molly and Christian both started to speak at once, to protest, but Dan raised his hand to shut it down.

"It's done. Gramps left me that house. There's a bedroom on the first floor there too, if I recall, and a decent kitchen. I can hire Mrs. O'Brien to air it out for me and there's a covered walkway between here and the house, so I can move between the two buildings safely. No potholes."

Christian grimaced at that. "I'm so sorry, I don't know how the hell that got there."

"Don't be ridiculous. I was the dumb one walking in the dark."

Molly spoke up then and Dan caught a sense of excitement in her voice. "I have a great idea! Since you're going to be here for a while longer now, why don't you hire Traci to decorate the house for you, make it your own? It'll only increase the value of the place if you decide to sell."

Dan's first reaction was no. He wasn't going to be here long-term, so why bother to redecorate? He was about to say as much when something stopped him. He realized he actually liked the idea. It would give him something else to focus on and to do with his time, and he could hang out with Traci without Christian's disapproval.

"That's actually not a bad idea."

Traci wasn't having second thoughts about breaking up with Billy, but she was missing him a little. They did have some good times together and he was always good about remembering birthdays and anniversaries. She supposed that was why she was feeling a little blue. Today was November 10, and would have been the second anniversary of their first date. Billy had made a big fuss about it last year and would have likely done so again if they were still together.

She had just walked in the door a few minutes before and was supposed to be meeting her brother in a half hour at their mother's house for dinner. It was busy at the store all day and she was exhausted and much more in the mood to climb into her sweats and crawl into bed, but she hadn't seen her mother in a few weeks and didn't want to cancel last minute. It was only a ten minute drive, so she could relax for a few minutes before she had to go. She was just about to collapse on the sofa when there was a soft knock at the door. She sighed as she walked over and peeked out the window. She really didn't even need to look; her gut had told her who it was.

"Happy anniversary." Billy was standing outside, looking cold. At least he wasn't holding flowers this time.

"Hi, Billy."

"I don't suppose I can come in for a minute?" he asked hopefully. Traci was actually tempted. What harm could it do? But, she didn't want to give him the wrong idea- to think she was softening, because she wasn't.

"I'm actually heading out in a minute, dinner at my parents."

"Oh, okay. Well, I just wanted you to know I was thinking of you. It would have been our anniversary today, you know."

"I know," she said softly, then added, "Take care of yourself, Billy."

Traci shut the door and then curled up on the sofa, wrapped in her favorite fleece throw, fighting the tears that threatened to spill over. She didn't want to be with Billy. She was glad she'd ended things; but still, it was hard, especially on days like this when she was reminded that it would have been two years and they were on track to be married in less than six months. The phone rang and she slowly got up and shuffled over to it, hoping it wasn't Billy again.

"Traci?" It was a man's voice, familiar and yet strange. She wasn't sure who it was.

"Yes, it's Traci."

"This is Dan. Dan Ford?" This was interesting, and unexpected.

"Hi, Dan. What's up?"

"Well, it turns out that I'm going to be staying here a few months longer than anticipated and so I'll be moving into the guest house here at the ranch. I don't know if you'd be interested, but I'm thinking about doing some renovating, redecorating actually, and Molly suggested I give you a call?"

"Oh, I'd love to! When were you thinking?"

"As soon as you're available. As soon as tomorrow, even."

"I'm working tomorrow, but day after should work. I can meet you there at about ten if that's good."

"That's great, see you then."

Traci hung up the phone and immediately felt her mood lift. She had a new project and would be spending some time with Dan. There was something about him that just made her feel happy. He was easy to be with and there was no pressure; he had made it very clear that he'd be heading back to Chicago as soon as possible. Plus, she found him extremely attractive, there was a certain spark or chemistry, whatever you wanted to call it. All she knew is she felt a pull to be around him and because she knew it couldn't go anywhere, and there were no expectations of anything on either side. It didn't make her nervous. It was fun having a totally harmless crush. It was just what she needed right now.

Chapter Six

Two days later, Traci pulled into the driveway at the ranch, gathered her notebook and laptop and made her way to the guesthouse, which was directly next to the main house. It was quite a bit smaller, and there was a covered walk-way between the two buildings. Once she reached the front door, she didn't even need to knock. Dan had seen her coming and held the door open.

"Thanks for coming on such short notice," he said. "Come on into the kitchen. We can sit here and talk." He led Traci through the family room, which had an oversized, wood-burning fire place and into the kitchen which was rustic and opened into a generous sized eating area. It was separated by an L-shaped island made of polished, dark pine and had stools on one side. In the corner of the room, a black, cast-iron wood-stove had a crackling fire going that was throwing out some good heat. Traci shrugged off her jacket and slipped it over the back of a chair.

"Coffee? I just made a big pot." Dan pulled a mug from a cabinet above the coffee-maker and waited to hear if Traci would join him.

"Sure, I'll have a cup. Just black, please, no sugar." Dan poured two cups, added milk and sugar to his and then Traci jumped up and brought them over to the table, since she couldn't imagine how he could carry even one cup of coffee, let alone two while using crutches. They both sat down at the table, across from each other, and then Dan started talking.

"So, not sure if you've already heard. It's a little embarrassing, but I managed to re-injure myself and will be here at least another few months, according to the doctor." He described how he'd hurt himself and Traci sympathized. She could picture him, excited to be almost done with recovery and feeling stronger and impulsively making a not-so-smart decision to take a walk in the dark.

"Don't beat yourself up about it. Honestly, it's something I could have seen myself doing."

"I was just feeling so restless, and wishing I was back in my own place. You can never really relax when you're visiting someone, even if it is family."

"I know what you mean. So, that's why you've moved in here then, to have some privacy and feel more at home?"

"Exactly. My grandfather left most of the ranch to my brother, which makes sense, as I've never had any interest in it. But, it was decent of him to leave me the guest house. I didn't think I'd have much use for it, but it's kind of funny how things turn out."

"So, what are you thinking you want to do here?" Traci opened her notebook and readied her pen to jot down ideas as they talked.

"Well, I have the time and the budget to make this place feel like home. As you may have noticed walking in here, it's kind of sparse, bare bones. It's been empty now for about a year. Before that, one of the ranch managers lived here for a number of years. He was single and never needed much. When he moved on, the new manager Christian hired lives a few miles up the road and has a big family, five kids and a couple of dogs, so he opted to stay where he is."

"So, it's been empty since then," Traci confirmed.

"Right. Mrs. O'Brien spent the day here yesterday, giving it a good cleaning and airing it out. First thing I need to do is order a bed. If you're free, I thought maybe we could take a drive into Bozeman so I could pick one out, and maybe we could look at some other furniture at the same time."

"Of course. We could go to Jason's Furniture. I get a lot of stuff there and the prices are reasonable. They're open late. We could go after work tonight or early tomorrow."

"I could do tonight any time after four. The stock market closes at two since I'm on the West coast and then I have a few things to do to finish up after that."

"What else are you thinking of doing here?" Traci looked around the room, wondering what he had in mind.

"Well, I need the basics, a few big screen TVs, comfortable sofas, and then I thought you could figure out the rest; do what you did at Christian's and at The Rose Garden."

"Drapes and accessories, things like that, you mean?" Traci wanted to be sure they were on the same page.

"Yeah, just make the place look nice, but not too girly. You know what to do. Christian's place looks great."

"Thanks. Yeah, I have a few ideas already. We should discuss your favorite colors, any that you dislike, kind of fabrics you prefer, if you like leather sofas or something else?" They went over Dan's likes and dislikes and Traci started to make a plan. She could already picture the look she wanted and couldn't wait to get started.

"When we go to Jason's later, you should be able to pick out a sofa and find a TV or two as well."

"At least two," Dan confirmed and Traci smiled. Of course two TVs, maybe even three. Guys seemed to like a TV in every room.

"Okay, I'll see you back here a little after four, then."

Dan was still sleeping in the main house, until he could get a new bed delivered. But, he'd gone ahead and moved all of his office stuff over, setting up his laptops on the kitchen table, so he'd be in easy reach of everything he needed. Mrs. O'Brien had stocked the refrigerator there as well, and had offered to add a few hours to her week to look after Dan's place in addition to the main house. He gratefully accepted that offer, an admission that he did enjoy being fussed over a bit.

He got his blog and video done earlier than usual, so he'd be ready to go as soon as Traci arrived. He was looking forward to their trip to Bozeman and, admittedly, to spending more time with her. Although Dan hadn't dated anyone seriously in several years, he did date often and he was now into his third month without a date of any kind, unless he counted going to Isabella's opening with Traci, which wasn't really a date; so he wasn't counting it. Besides, Traci was off-limits for dating, given that his brother would kill him if he started something that he couldn't finish and he liked Traci too much to mess up what was beginning to be a nice friendship. He could be friends and still like looking at her, right? Even though he was, in fact, very attracted to Traci. But who wouldn't be? She was a very pretty girl, not jaw-dropping beautiful like Isabella, but those kinds of looks usually came with their own challenges. He liked looking at Traci, with her long, shiny dark hair that fell just past her shoulders and was cut into wavy layers that framed her face, big brown eyes and a small nose covered with freckles that he found cute and that she probably hated. He grinned at the thought of it and then turned at the sound of a car coming down the driveway. He grabbed his crutches and made his way to the window. It wasn't Traci, not yet; it was Molly home from the Inn. But, a moment later, another car pulled in and this looked like Traci's car, a white Ford Escape.

Dan grabbed his crutches and was just about at the door when there was a knock, and it was Traci.

"I saw you pull in," he said as he opened the door.

"Are you ready to go?"

"Looking forward to it." He shut the door carefully behind him and then followed Traci to the car and handed her his crutches which she stowed in the back seat.

They chatted comfortably on the way to Bozeman. Traci told him about the store and how they were starting to get busy now that the holidays were around the corner. Dan quickly changed the subject at the first mention of the holidays and Traci happily followed his lead.

Dan was surprised at how busy the furniture store was when they arrived and wondered if it was early holiday traffic.

"No, it's always like this," Traci said. "This is the biggest furniture store in the state and they keep expanding. The whole bottom floor is a discount outlet. I picked up a gorgeous cream sofa there for next to nothing. It was in perfect condition except for a barely noticeable pen mark."

"They have a 3-D theater?" Dan commented as Traci drove through the parking lot.

"Yes. It's very clever of them, really. They give out free hot dogs and have short 3D films playing so the whole family will come, and stay and buy. They make it easy with all kinds of financing and crazy specials."

Once they parked, Traci jumped out and got Dan's crutches out of the back seat and handed them to him. They made their way inside and first strolled through the giant discount outlet, but Dan didn't see anything that he had to have. They took an escalator up one level, to the main showroom and Traci led him into a huge, dark room filled with a selection of leather sofas and chairs. This was more like it. A few styles caught his eye and he and Traci sat on all of them until he found the one that he didn't want to get up from. It was an oversized, chocolate brown leather that was buttery soft and had just the right amount of give so that you could sink into it but still have some support. He chose a chair that matched as well, and then Traci led him to a gorgeous, polished pine bar with matching swivel chairs. It would look perfect in the corner of the family room.

Next up was the office section, where he picked out an oversized desk that would comfortably hold his multiple monitors and a solid chair to match. Dan was impressed by how quickly they were getting things done. In the home entertainment section, with its selection of big screen TVs, Dan picked out three, in varying sizes, for the family room, bedroom and office. Last on the list was picking out a bed. Traci led him into the biggest showroom they'd seen yet, with a dizzying array of beds of all sizes.

"Do you know what style you want? Pillow-top, plush, or firm?"

"I have no idea. I've never picked out a bed before."

"Even for your place in Chicago?"

"I bought that place furnished, and it included an almost new bed. It's comfortable enough. Not sure what category it would fit into, though."

"Okay, we'll just have to try a few out, then," Traci said with a smile and Dan's mind immediately went to a very different place.

"Lead the way."

Traci brought him to a king-sized bed that had a thick pillow-top and he sat down and then laid back. It was like floating on a cloud. "Join me," he said with a smile.

"Don't be silly. It's your bed," Traci laughed.

"No, seriously, I want your opinion, too."

"Okay." Traci tentatively climbed onto the other side of the bed and stretched out.

"Oh, this is nice."

Dan was thinking the same thing, but he wasn't thinking about the bed as much as the idea of Traci lying next to him. He got up quickly and moved to the next bed. They made their way around the entire room, testing out each bed. The overwhelming winner was the first one they had tried. Dan pulled out his credit card to pay and made arrangements to have everything delivered a few days later.

"That was almost too easy," he said as they walked out.

"It's a fun place, isn't it? I had a feeling you'd like it here."

"Have you eaten yet?" Dan asked as they reached the car.

"No, not yet."

"I'd like to buy you dinner to thank you for helping me."

"I never say no to food," Traci said with a smile as they got settled into the car.

"You know this area better than I do. Any favorite places nearby?"

Traci thought for a moment. "Yes, there's a good steakhouse at the edge of town, on our way back. Lou's Tavern."

"Sounds good to me."

Fifteen minutes later they were seated at a table at Lou's. When the waitress came, Traci ordered a glass of wine and Dan got a local beer, an IPA on tap. The menu was short and sweet and they both ordered sirloin steaks with baked potato and salad. A few minutes after they placed their orders, the waitress returned with their salads and they started eating.

"So, how are you doing?" Dan asked. "Your ex isn't giving you any trouble, is he?" Dan didn't like what he'd seen of Billy and hoped that Traci was being smart and staying clear of him.

"I'm good. I saw Billy briefly a few days ago. He stopped

by the house to say 'hi'. It would have been our anniversary and I think that day was hard for both of us." Dan didn't like the sound of that and must have made a face because Traci quickly continued.

"I didn't invite him in, if that's what you're worried about. I was on my way out to my mother's, so it worked out well." She hesitated a moment before adding, "Billy's really not that bad."

Dan wasn't convinced. "Good thing you didn't invite him in. That might have given him false hopes."

Traci sighed. "I know. I didn't want to encourage him. He still seems to be hoping I'll change my mind." When Dan said nothing in response to that, Traci added, "I'm not going to."

The waitress brought their steaks out a few minutes later and they were cooked perfectly. They dug in and chatted about everything and nothing while they ate and then to Dan's dismay, the subject of the holidays came up again.

"I'm so glad it's almost the holidays. It's my favorite time of year and it will help get my mind off the breakup with Billy. I volunteer at our church, managing the Christmas pageant, and they have me handling all the Christmas promotions at the store as well." Traci's face lit up as she spoke and Dan had to force himself to keep his expression neutral. The less he said, the sooner they could talk about something else. "And I have to find the perfect Santa for the annual Christmas pictures. That starts in two weeks, the first Saturday after Thanksgiving."

"You just need to find an old fat guy with white hair, right?" he commented and even cracked a smile.

"It's more than that. I need to find someone who has the

right personality, who really feels the magic of Christmas. You know?"

"Sure." He popped another bite of steak in his mouth and glanced around the room. She had to be just about done with the holiday talk.

Instead, surprising him, she asked, "What's wrong?"

"What do you mean?" he asked cautiously.

"You seem to shut down when I start talking about Christmas and the holiday season. I take it you don't get quite as excited about it as I do," she said gently.

He avoided directly answering the question. "I get excited about New Year's Eve."

"Oh, you like to count down to the New Year? Drink champagne?"

It was time to put an end to it. "I like New Year's Eve because it means that the holiday season is over."

Traci looked disappointed at that. "You really don't like the holidays? Why?"

Dan hesitated. He and his brother were so different in this regard. Christian loved the holidays and loved to make as big of a fuss as his parents and grandparents used to. It had always been a huge deal in their house. Christmas lights everywhere, huge Christmas tree, and on Christmas Eve, an open house that all of their families and friends would attend. It lasted for hours and there were people coming and going all night, and so much food and love. It hurt still to even think about how things used to be.

"Dan? You okay?" Traci sounded far away and Dan realized he'd drifted off for a moment.

"Bad memories," he said simply, and then saw Traci's face flush as she connected the dots.

"I'm so sorry. Your parents. It's been so long, but I still remember, and can't imagine how awful it must have been for you two."

"It was a long time ago, but it still hurts to think about it. They were on their way back from the market, with a carload of groceries for the open house that night. A drunk driver slammed into them on Christmas Eve, of all nights." They were both quiet for a moment, and then he added, "So, I hope you can understand why I just like to lay low and sort of get through the holidays."

"I suppose. It is awful what happened to your parents." Traci took a sip of wine and seemed to be considering whether or not to say something. Finally, she spoke. "I understand why you don't like to make a fuss about the holidays. But, your parents loved them. That party was something they loved to do and it was something they shared with everyone. Do you think, maybe, they'd want you to try and enjoy the time a bit more?"

"They're dead. I don't know what they think anymore," Dan snapped, and then regretted it as he saw the hurt look on Traci's face.

"I wish I could enjoy the holidays the way I used to, the way Christian does and you do, but I just can't. Truthfully, I hate this time of year. I dread it, and can't get through it fast enough. Sorry to be such a downer." He smiled then and hoped she would understand.

"No worries. It will get easier for you, eventually," she

said, and then added thoughtfully, "Maybe being back here will help."

"Maybe," Dan agreed as he was thinking, 'no way in hell.' He attempted to change the subject again. "Feel like splitting a piece of chocolate cake? I saw one go by and it looks pretty good."

Traci smiled, and said, "It's beyond good."

The waitress cleared their plates and brought out a piece of cake and two forks.

"So, what's next? Painting?" Dan asked. He had initially told Traci that he wanted to give the whole place a re-do, so that it felt more like home.

"Yes. I can drop by in the next day or two and we can pick colors. I've got a bunch of paint samples I can show you."

"Oh, I trust you, whatever you think will look good. I don't know anything about that stuff."

"Well, I have a few ideas in mind, so I'll show you those and how they look in different light, and then once the walls are all done, then we'll choose the window treatments and accessories."

After they finished the cake, Traci drove home and they decided to meet at the same time the next day.

Dan watched Traci drive away as he let himself into the house. At least if he was going to be stuck here for a while, he'd be able to spend more time with Traci. She was very different from the girls he usually went out with in Chicago.

Chapter Seven

The following morning Traci met Molly at the Morning Muffin at eight a.m. for breakfast. The Morning Muffin was one of only two breakfast places in town and, due to its central Main Street location and killer scones, it was also the busiest. Molly was already there when Traci arrived, so she got in line at the counter and a few minutes later brought her coffee and triple-berry glazed scone to Molly's table.

"Thanks for meeting me on such short notice," Molly said as Traci settled into her seat.

"I don't have to be in until nine, so it works out perfectly. How did you manage to get away?" Molly usually served breakfast at the Inn.

"My aunt and mom are managing without me. They like helping out and I was ready for a break."

"How's everything going? Are you busy still, now that Isabella is open?" Molly had a strong background in hotel management, so Traci knew she'd do a great job with The Rose Cottage, but it must have been frustrating to have Christian's ex-girlfriend open a similar bed and breakfast so soon after.

"It's going surprisingly well. We're steady." Molly paused for a moment and Traci thought she saw a gleam of mischief in her eyes. She was debating whether or not to ask her about it when Molly started talking again. "So, the funniest thing happened the other night. You know how I was mentioning that I would never run a splashy opening special like the one she ran, the buy one night, get one free deal?" Traci nodded. "Well, guess who called me late that Friday night in a panic wondering if I could put up a few of her guests, on her?"

"You're kidding? What happened?"

"An issue with the water heater. No hot water for several of their rooms, and no one available to fix it until the following Monday. Ironically, two of the parties were guests who had cancelled their reservations with me to take advantage of her special."

"I almost feel bad for Isabella," Traci said.

Molly chuckled, and then said, "I definitely felt bad for her. I wouldn't wish that on anyone. But it is funny how karma has a way of taking care of things."

"I'm glad to hear that things are going well for you." Traci was happy for Molly as she seemed so passionate about The Rose Cottage.

"Thanks. I'm having a lot of fun with it. How are things going with you?How's it going with Dan's decorating project?"

Traci took a bite of her scone before answering. It was so good and she was savoring every bite.

"So far, so good. We went into Bozeman after work yesterday and picked out some new furniture, sofas, TVs, that kind of thing. Tonight I'm stopping over with some paint samples to pick out colors for his walls."

"Will he want something similar to Christian's look, do you think?" Molly spread cream cheese on the other half of her bagel while Traci considered the question.

"I don't think so. He said he admired the way Christian's decorating looks, but I get the sense he might be more of a minimalist, wanting more of a sleek look, to remind him of the city. I could be wrong, of course, but it's just a vibe I get. He has no clutter, is very organized and has said how much he loves living in Chicago."

"Yeah, Christian said that he was lucky if Dan made it back once a year, usually around Thanksgiving and it was always just for the long weekend, and then he'd be gone. He never comes for Christmas."

"That doesn't surprise me. We talked about it a little and it's not his favorite time of year."

Molly frowned before she took another sip of coffee."-Because of what happened to his parents? I can understand that."

"Yes, but it's been so long. And from what he said, Christian is the complete opposite. He loves Christmas, like I do."

"It's hard to imagine not loving the holidays," Molly agreed.

"Maybe it will be different for him this year, since he'll be here." Traci wished that she could somehow help Dan feel the same sense of joy that she always felt and looked forward to this time of year.

"Maybe, though it may be even harder for him with everyone around him so into it," Molly said thoughtfully.

"You've spent time with both of them, with Dan living in the house. Do they seem similar to you?"

"Dan and Christian? No, not at all. Christian is so settled. He knows what he wants to do and where he wants to be and he loves his life here. Dan is great, he's fun and friendly." She paused for a moment as if trying to find the right words. "But I think he seems a bit lost, like he's still trying to find his way. Don't get me wrong, he's crazy smart and obviously successful and very good at what he does, but he doesn't seem as settled. He's very much a bachelor. Christian said he hasn't been serious about anyone in years and that he runs with somewhat of a fast crowd, or as he put it, 'surface people'. They're more into how they look and how others see them."

"Really? What do you mean?" This didn't seem to fit what Traci knew of Dan based on the time they'd spent together thus far.

"His friends are movers and shakers in the finance world, and they mostly date models or young trust fund society types who don't work but go to all the right charity events and parties. He's out almost every night, and usually with a different girl."

For some reason, Traci found that thought depressing. It didn't sound like a fun way to live to her, not all the time anyway.

"I didn't know that," she said.

"Yeah, and most of his friends have stopped calling. The first week it was non-stop. Then as soon as they realized that Dan wasn't going to be around for a while, they moved on. I'm sure they're mostly nice people, but it's out of sight out of mind, it seems. I think he's feeling a little lonely and probably frustrated. This latest injury really set him back. He was hoping to be home by now."

"I wonder if he'll sell his place once he goes back. It seems a shame to put so much into it, redecorating and all, if he's not going to keep it."

"Hard to say. Wouldn't surprise me if he decides to sell. It doesn't really make sense to keep a place that you only visit one long weekend a year. Plus, he's got plenty of money, so it's a good project for him, like the Rose Cottage was for me. It keeps us busy until it's time to go home."

"I suppose." Traci didn't like to think of Molly leaving either. Her six months would be up soon and then she'd be free to return to Manhattan and to the promotion for her dream job at the Clarendon Hotel.

"How are you doing?" Molly asked. "Are you thinking of dating anyone? Things are definitely over with Billy, right?"

"Dating anyone? No." Traci shuddered at the thought. She wasn't ready to date again. It was definitely too soon. "Yes, things are over with Billy. I'm not sure if that's registered with him yet, but I'm not going back there again."

"Well, when you least expect it, you'll probably meet someone. You know the saying about finding love when you stop looking for it?"

"Yes, but I'm not in any hurry for it to find me." Traci

laughed as she glanced at her watch and then stood up. "I have to fly to get to work on time. Tell your mom and aunt I said hi."

"Will do. We'll have you and Travis over again soon for dinner."

"Sounds great. Talk to you soon."

Chapter Eight

I made you a nice tray of lasagna and left it in the fridge. All you have to do is throw it in the oven to heat up. It's already cooked." Mrs. O'Brien stood in the shadow of Dan's computer monitors, and he knew that she was ready to leave for the day. Dan was hunched behind his bank of computer screens, intent on his work. But he looked up as soon as he'd sensed her waiting.

"Thanks a million. I really appreciate it."

Mrs. O'Brien scowled at him. "Well, don't forget to eat it. You're starting to look skinny."

Dan smiled at that. "No worries there, I'm starving already."

"Okay, then, I'm on my way. I'll see you tomorrow," Mrs. O'Brien said.

Dan wished her a good night and then she was gone.

He checked the time; Traci was due in about a half hour. If he rushed, he could get both his video and blog posts done and then he could relax and enjoy her company. The day had mostly dragged and he couldn't wait to see Traci. He'd been looking forward to it all day. He couldn't put his finger on what it was about her. No doubt it was partly because she was off-limits, but it was more than that. He'd felt drawn to her since they met and he was happy to spend whatever time he could with her, even if it had to be in a business capacity.

Exactly thirty minutes later, there was a soft knock at the door just as Dan was clicking send on his evening emails with the video and blog posts. He reached for his crutches and made his way to the door quickly. He was getting faster on them and he was feeling stronger, but was also more cautious this time. He opened the door, and Traci was standing there looking damn cute. She was wearing a bright red sweater dress with a long strand of creamy white pearls and had her hair tied back in a shimmery white scarf.

"You look great!" he said impulsively and she smiled.

"Thanks. Today was our first store-wide meeting about the holiday season, it seemed appropriate."

"Well, you look very festive." He grinned, and opened the door wide. "Come on in."

"I brought my sample book, so we can go over the different color options," Traci said as she walked in.

"Come on in the kitchen. You can set that on the island. The light is good there." Traci followed him into the kitchen and then spread the samples out across the island counter-top.

"So, I thought we'd go with mostly neutrals downstairs,

rich creams and soft caramel browns, and then some deeper blues and greens in the bedrooms and baths."

Dan had told Traci on their first meetings what his favorite colors were and what she was suggesting sounded fine by him.

"Like I said, whatever you think sounds good works for me."

"Okay. Well, we should still bring these samples upstairs to make sure you like the way look in those rooms." Traci dug out several samples and waited for Dan to lead the way upstairs.

"Sure, let's go." He was getting better at using his crutches on the stairs and there was only one flight to the second floor so it wasn't too bad.

They came to the bathrooms first and Traci held up the different colors that she had in mind and he nodded appreciatively. Then they went into the guest bedroom, which she had selected a soft misty green shade for and once again he confirmed that it looked fine. Lastly, they came back downstairs to the master bedroom, which looked large and lonely with its simple double bed that was left over from the last tenant.

For this room, Traci had selected a deep, silvery bluish gray color that he would never have picked out for himself, but when she held the color sample up against the wall, he was impressed by how well it worked and how restful it looked.

"You really do know your stuff."

"So, you like it?"

"Love it! Did you really have any doubt?" He was surprised to see that she looked relieved. As if there'd been any question.

"Well, you never do know." She smiled then. "I'm so glad you like it. While the painting is getting done, I'll start picking out fabric swatches so we can start on the window treatments. And I think Jose, the guy I usually suggest for painting, can start tomorrow, so he'll probably be done before your furniture arrives."

"Wow, you don't mess around. I like that." Dan was impressed that Traci was getting things done so quickly, but on the other hand, he was a little dismayed, too...he didn't want her to finish up too fast. The longer it took, the more she'd be around.

"So, do you have plans for dinner? Mrs. O'Brien made lasagna."

Traci looked disappointed. "That sounds wonderful, but I can't stay. I have to run to a meeting at the church. Planning for the Christmas pageant is about to start."

"Oh, okay. Another time, then." He could always bring the lasagna over to the main house and visit with Molly and Christian, but he couldn't help feeling disappointed. He'd been looking forward to hanging out with Traci for a few hours and enjoying a good homemade meal.

"I'll stop by tomorrow after work, though, to see how it's coming along. Maybe there will be some leftovers we could share?" she suggested.

"Oh, absolutely. Mrs. O'Brien makes enough for an army." His mood suddenly brighter, he walked Traci to the door and then put a call into the main house and minutes later, Molly popped over to grab the lasagna and he followed her over.

·❦·

"So, what were you looking so happy about?" Molly asked Dan once they were all seated around the kitchen table. She had popped the lasagna in the oven to heat up while Christian opened a couple of beers and handed one to Dan. Molly helped herself to some salad, while she waited for Dan to respond.

"Just happy with the work Traci is doing. She's amazing."

Christian frowned at him as Molly grinned. She took a sip of her red wine and then added, "Yeah, she is isn't she?"

"Behave yourself," Christian said as he reached for a slice of bread.

"I've been on my best behavior," Dan said.

"Speaking of best behavior, do you want to join Christian at the wine dinner this weekend? He was going to meet Travis and Traci there, but Travis can't go now, so there's an extra ticket."

"Is this a set up?" Dan teased.

"Hardly," Christian snapped.

"Lighten up, I'm just kidding," he said to his brother and then smiled at Molly.

"I'd love to, sounds fun."

"Great, I think you'll enjoy it. I'm using the caterer that did Isabella's BBQ, and the food will be amazing. It should be a good time."

Chapter Nine

Traci saw Molly's mother and Aunt Betty already seated in the hospitality room when she arrived at St. David's. There was a plate of chocolate chip cookies in the middle of the table and about a dozen women were chatting over cups of coffee while they waited for a few others to arrive. Aunt Betty waved her over as she walked in and indicated that the seat next to her was free. Traci settled into the chair and helped herself to a cookie, as she was starving.

"I just made those, right before we came over," Aunt Betty said.

Traci inhaled the cookie, and reached for another. "They're amazing, thanks for bringing them."

"It's nothing. We can't have a meeting without something sweet, right?"

"Sounds like a good policy to me," Traci agreed.

A few minutes later, everyone had arrived and settled in and Traci started the meeting. This was the third year that she was chairing the Christmas pageant. It went so well the first time she did it that it was understood that she'd be taking it on each year. She didn't mind, though. As she'd told Dan earlier, Traci loved Christmas. She appreciated the significance of it, of course, but it was more than that. She loved that special feeling that was in the air, the anticipation of something magical and special and the happy glow that stretched from Thanksgiving to New Year's Day and was reinforced by Christmas carols and general merriment.

Jim, the music director, spoke for a bit about his thoughts for background music and Traci followed with details on the list of parts and available children to participate. They liked to include all the children that were interested in being a part of the pageant and there were opportunities for the shy ones as well who didn't want a speaking part but loved the idea of wearing a costume and being a supporting player. They were able to cover everything in about an hour and as they were cleaning up after the meeting, Molly's mom spoke up.

"What are you and your family doing for Thanksgiving, Traci? Molly and Christian and Dan are coming to our place and we'd love to have you and Travis and your parents join us, if you don't already have plans?"

"So nice of you to think of us. My mother might love that idea, actually, as it's usually just the four of us. I'll see her soon and let you know as soon as possible." She was 99% sure her mother would jump at the chance to have someone else do all the cooking, and it would be a fun change to be with a bigger group on the holiday, especially when they were her friends.

As she was walking out to her car, someone called her name and Traci froze. She'd been looking down, focused on where she was going and hadn't even noticed Billy walking towards her.

"What are you doing here?" she asked, surprised to see him, although he was also a member of the church.

"Men's group meets tonight. I'm here a little early as it's my turn to cook. We're doing ribs...at least, that's what Jim said he was bringing. I'm just the cook."

"Oh, okay, right. Forgot you were in men's group." Truthfully, Traci hadn't even given Billy a thought in recent days.

"How've you been? You look great, as usual." He smiled his slightly crooked grin, the one she used to find so charming. Now, it didn't really affect her at all.

"I'm good, thanks. You?" Traci wished she didn't feel so awkward now talking with Billy, but he still had that hopeful look in his eyes and she had to fight the urge to run and to instead stay calm and be polite.

"So, when do I report for Santa duty? Same as last year?"

Traci's heart sank. She'd almost forgotten that she'd asked Billy to be the store Santa again. To his credit, he filled in last year and did a great job. The kids loved him, and Traci had impulsively locked him in almost a year ago. It had crossed her mind a few weeks back, and she was going to suggest to Billy then that it might not be a great idea, but she'd chickened out, and then it had slipped her mind again. So, she was stuck with Billy. It was probably too late at this point to find another Santa anyway, and Billy was planning on doing it every weekend between Thanksgiving and Christmas.

"Yes, we'll have a quick meeting Saturday morning after Thanksgiving, before the store opens, and then you're on for the rest of the day."

"Perfect. I'll see you then."

As Billy walked away, Traci told herself that it would be fine. Billy seemed relatively normal now; maybe he was finally starting to accept that things were over. Plus, he'd be way too busy at the store to cause any issues. That Saturday especially, being right after the crazy day after Thanksgiving madness and the first official visit with Santa, was going to be non-stop all day.

Traci couldn't believe that Thanksgiving was right around the corner and with it, the start of the holiday season. She was excited about the idea of spending the holiday with a bigger group, and if she was being truthful, she really liked that Dan would be there. She hoped that this year might be less dark for him, that spending the holidays with friends and family might lighten his mood and help him get through what was usually a difficult time of year.

She was looking forward to seeing him tomorrow night, too, to check on the progress of the painting and if he was still interested in sharing some of his leftover lasagna. She made a mental note to herself to pick up a good bottle of red wine to bring along for dinner. She then reminded herself that she shouldn't feel so excited about seeing him again; after all, it's not like they were dating. It was strictly business.

The next day did not fly by. The store wasn't very busy, which always made time go by more slowly, and it didn't help that Traci kept glancing at the clock, willing it to go faster. When five o'clock finally rolled around, she grabbed her purse and headed to Dan's. She stopped along the way at a small wine shop, and picked out a bottle of merlot to have with the lasagna. Although this was strictly a business meeting, they were having dinner and she couldn't help feeling a bit of nervous anticipation. She reminded herself again that this was not a date. But, would it be so bad if it was? She realized that she was thinking of Dan in a way that wasn't very professional. But, it wouldn't be right to go there, for multiple reasons. Still, it was harmless to daydream and to flirt a bit.

She pulled into the driveway and gathered her purse and the wine and then made her way to the front door. She was about to knock when the door opened and Dan was standing there, looking adorable. He was in jeans and a blue plaid flannel shirt and had a hint of stubble, a look she'd always found appealing.

"I heard the car pull up," he explained as held the door open for her to come in.

She handed him the wine and took off her coat, draping it over a kitchen chair, where she also set her purse.

"Jose just left a few minutes ago. He had two guys with him and they blasted through. Said they just need a half-day tomorrow to finish up the trim."

"Really? That's great! He always does a good job."

"Ready to take a look? I'll lead the way." Dan moved quickly on his crutches and Traci followed along as he pointed out the progress in each room. The colors they'd picked look amazing. Traci always got a thrill seeing the shades she chose go from tiny scraps of color to full blown glory on the walls. The overall look was both soft and masculine at the same time.

"You're really good at this color thing," Dan said with a smile. "I had no idea it would make such a difference."

They were standing in the master bedroom and Traci tried to picture the furniture Dan had bought against the soothing shade of misty blue-gray. There was a new bedding set that had just come into the store a few days ago. It would look perfect against this color, she realized.

"Do you need sheets, comforters, pillows, or do you already have all that?" she asked.

Dan looked confused for a moment and then chuckled. "I don't have any of that. I could probably borrow a set of sheets from Christian, but should really get my own, I suppose."

"Good, I can take care of that if you like." Traci told him about the set she had in mind and Dan was more than happy to have her get whatever else she thought he needed.

"Are you hungry?" Dan asked as they made their way back to the kitchen.

"Yes, that smells amazing."

"I put the lasagna in to heat up. It should be just about ready."

"Can I do anything to help?"

"Sure, there's a wine opener in this drawer if you want to open the wine and pour us some." While Dan was getting the lasagna out of the oven, Traci opened the wine, found the wine glasses and poured a glass for each of them. Dan piled generous helpings of the steaming pasta onto a couple of plates and Traci carried them over to the kitchen table and then returned with their wine glasses.

They chatted easily through dinner and then as they were just about finished, Dan asked, "Do you have to rush home for anything?"

"No, I'm not in any hurry to be anywhere. No other meetings tonight." She smiled at that and wondered why he was asking.

"When I was flipping channels last night I stumbled onto a movie on demand that looks pretty good. It was too late to start watching it last night, so I was planning on seeing it tonight. I'd love the company, if you're interested?" He mentioned the name of the movie and it was one Traci had planned to see but never got around to, so she knew she'd like it. But, she would have been happy to stay, regardless.

"Sure, I meant to see that when it was playing in the theaters but never got around to it."

Dan topped their glasses off with a bit more wine and Traci carried them into the other room, where they settled onto the old, worn sofa that Dan was using until his new stuff arrived. There was a soft throw blanket that she snuggled under and got comfortable as the movie started.

They didn't talk much during the movie, but Traci was very aware of Dan sitting less than a foot away. The movie was a comedy and they both enjoyed it. It was still early when the movie finished, so Traci didn't object when Dan clicked onto a new film, this time a suspense thriller. About half-way through, though, her eyes started getting heavy as she was so warm and cozy under the throw blanket and was starting to feel the effects of the lasagna and wine. She remembered thinking that she should really probably head home when the next thing she knew, a soft voice was whispering in her ear, "Traci, are you awake?"

She snapped to attention and realized she'd fallen fast asleep and was snuggled up against Dan. How mortifying!

"I can't believe I fell asleep! What time is it? I should go." The words came out in a rush.

"It's not that late. I wasn't sure if you were asleep or not. I think you just dozed for a little bit. I put the movie on pause."

Traci jumped up. "I'm so glad you woke me. I should head out."

"Are you sure? You're welcome to crash on the couch if you like."

"I'm fine. I'm awake now. I only had about a glass and a half of wine, so I'm okay to drive. It's just been a long week and I think I fell into a bit of a food coma."

"Mrs. O'Brien's lasagna is known to have that effect on people." Dan stood and walked over to where Traci was pulling on her coat and getting her keys out of her purse.

"I'm glad you stayed. It was fun hanging out with you."

"You mean as I fell asleep? Great company," Traci laughed, but was a bit embarrassed.

"You were only asleep for a few minutes. You're welcome to fall asleep here anytime." Dan pulled her in for a goodbye hug and surprised her with a kiss on her forehead.

"Drive careful. When will you be back?"

Traci thought for a moment. She could pick up the bedding tomorrow and the furniture would be coming at some point, too, and he'd need the sheets for his bed, as the one he was sleeping on now wasn't the same size.

"I'll call you towards the end of the day tomorrow and if the furniture is all in, I can swing by with your bedding and see how it all looks."

"Perfect, see you tomorrow." Dan closed the door and Traci drove home wishing his kiss had landed somewhere other than her forehead.

Chapter Ten

The next morning, Dan was over at the main house, as usual, having his morning coffee with Molly and Christian before they all headed out for the day. Christian was upstairs and Molly was puttering around the kitchen, making toast, while Dan sat at the island bar, sipping his second cup of rich, dark roast coffee. He was idly glancing at the paper, when the phone rang and Molly answered. He didn't pay much attention, as the call was for her and none of his business, but he couldn't help noticing how her tone changed and that she suddenly sounded very excited about something. He caught the tail end of a sentence as Molly walked out of the room for privacy. "The earliest I could start would be a month from now."

A few minutes later, she returned to the kitchen, set down the cordless phone and started buttering the toast that was likely cold by now. She said nothing about the phone call, and Dan didn't ask. After all, it wasn't any of his business. He couldn't help but wonder, though, if Christian might consider it his business to know where Molly might be heading off to in a month. He'd wait a bit first before saying anything, though, to see if she spoke to Christian on her own.

Traci called and came by later that evening as the painters had finished, and the furniture arrived on schedule. He had to admit, the place was looking sharp now that it was fully painted and full of furniture. The bedding that Traci had picked out looked great in his bedroom. It was a coordinated set of sheets, pillows and comforter in varying shades of dark blue and gray. He invited Traci to stay and visit, and was thinking they could order take-out, but she had to run off to another meeting at her church for that Christmas show she was involved with. Dan typically tuned out when the topic shifted to anything Christmas, but the gist of it was that she was busy. But, he'd be seeing her at the wine dinner the next night.

At breakfast the next morning, it was as if the phone call had never happened. Molly was her usual, cheerful self and Christian told him about a deal that was about to close and something with the farm. He didn't seem the least distracted or tense, so Dan suspected that Molly hadn't mentioned the phone call yet, and that bothered him. He didn't want to get involved in something that didn't concern him, but he knew his brother well enough to know he was falling hard for Molly, and that he didn't like surprises. Whatever Molly was up to, Christian deserved to know.

Later that evening, as they were in the car, heading to the wine dinner, Dan brought up the call and, as he suspected, Christian knew nothing about it.

"Are you sure that's what she said? That she could start in a month?"

"That's the only bit that I did hear, loud and clear. She sounded excited, too. It's probably that promotion she wanted, right?"

"Yeah. Strange that she hasn't mentioned it, though. You said the call was yesterday morning?"

"Right. I was having my morning coffee and you were upstairs getting dressed."

"And I never would have known if you hadn't mentioned it." Dan saw Christian's jaw clench and knew he was furious.

"I'm sure she would have mentioned it, eventually. She was probably waiting for the right moment." Dan liked Molly, so he wanted to give her the benefit of the doubt on this.

"Well, it seems like her mind is made up and she's just dreading tell me. Not sure how else you can spin this."

"Maybe it can still work out. You guys could do a long-distance relationship or something."

"Right. Like that would work. No, she's made up her mind, so that's it I guess. So be it."

They rode the rest of the way in silence as Dan didn't know what else to say and Christian didn't seem to be in the mood for small talk.

Traci was already there when they arrived and Dan was glad to see her. Christian was fuming and Dan wanted to diffuse the tension, and get him to relax and unwind. Molly was nowhere in sight and he figured she must be overseeing things in the kitchen. She'd explained at breakfast that she was using the same caterer Isabella had used for her BBQ over the summer as the food was so amazing and she was excited to see what she'd come up with for the wine dinner. One of the recipes was one of Molly's own family favorites, a lobster dish of some sort.

"Our table is over here." Traci led them to a round table that had little place cards with their names handwritten.

"Christian, why don't you have a seat and I'll get us some drinks? Traci, want to walk with me?" Christian sat, still in a bit of a daze as Dan and Traci made their way to the bar, where Dan ordered a round of drinks and Traci helped him carry them back to the table.

"Is Christian okay?" Traci whispered after they'd been sitting at the table for just a few minutes. It was that obvious that something was bothering Christian as he sat glowering into his drink. Dan had gotten him a Glenlivet on the rocks... he knew it would be a scotch kind of night for Christian.

"He's fine, just has a lot on his mind."

"Yeah, his work is crazy busy, right?"

"Always," Dan agreed, and figured it was best to let her think Christian's issue was work-related. She'd find out soon enough when Molly took off.

"Cheers!" Dan said, to change the subject and lift the mood. He clinked his glass against Christian's first and his brother barely lifted an eyebrow in response. Undeterred, he then shifted his attention to Traci and they tapped their glasses together. They were both sipping white wine. Dan figured since it was a wine dinner, why not stay with wine and they went with white because Molly had told them it was mostly seafood. He tried not to stare too often at Traci, who looked amazing in a sleek black dress that was very conservative in the front and dipped low in the back. It was sleeveless as well, and he couldn't help but admire her toned arms.

A short time later, the wine dinner got underway as waitresses brought out the first course, perfectly browned scallops over risotto and wine to match, followed by salads and then the entrees and a new wine, this time a buttery rich chardonnay which went well with the lobster casserole. They all chatted easily throughout the dinner and even Christian had loosened up a bit and moved on to wine from the scotch. Just when Dan was thinking he was over his initial fury and was starting to unwind, Christian got up from the table and said he'd be right back. Dan watched as he headed into the kitchen and figured nothing good would come from that visit.

But, Christian returned just a few minutes later and dug into the dessert that had just arrived.

"Did you say anything to her?" Dan asked.

"Not about the phone call. Timing wasn't right. Molly's back there doing all the cooking herself." Christian then explained that the caterer was sick and while Molly's mother and aunt took her home, Molly jumped in and handled all the cooking and plating of the food.

"Wow, that's impressive. Everything has gone so smoothly and the food is great. How did she ever manage that?"

"Guess that's her big hotel training taking over. They deal

with fires like this all the time. Doesn't hurt that she's a good cook, too."

"So, you'll talk to her later."

"Yeah, when she gets home."

Chapter Eleven

The next week was a tense one. The air was decidedly frosty when Dan went for coffee each morning. Christian had filled him in that the talk with Molly didn't go well. She was going back for the dream promotion in a month and Christian wouldn't consider a long-distance relationship. For him, it was over, and he didn't see the sense in dragging things out, so they ended things immediately. He thought it would be easier that way. Clearly, it wasn't. You could cut the tension in the air with a knife, so Dan didn't linger. He had his coffee, said his hellos and then went on his way.

Thanksgiving was in just a few days and they'd all be going to Molly's mother and aunt's place. He was looking forward to that, as Traci and Travis and their parents would be there as well, so it was bound to be a good time, or at least a bit more lively than it would be if they stayed home.

He hadn't seen Traci since the wine dinner a week ago, and was eager to see her. He'd gotten to like her stopping by every few days, but now that his place was done and decorated, there was no reason for her to keep visiting, unless he invited her over, which he hadn't done. He'd been thinking about it, though, and the idea was growing on him. She had to be over that Billy guy by now and maybe they could date and enjoy each other's company without getting too serious. Not that the idea of getting serious with Traci was a bad one, he just didn't think she wanted to get serious with anyone right away, especially someone who'd be moving back to Chicago soon. Funny, though, he was missing Chicago less and less these days. But, of course, he was looking forward to going back, after all that's where his life was, and all his friends. Though he hadn't heard from many of them lately, just the occasional message on Facebook and pictures of parties he would have been at. Chicago seemed very far away these days.

Thanksgiving morning came quickly, and as usual, Dan went to the main house for morning coffee. Thanksgiving was a holiday that he didn't mind all that much, except for its proximity to Christmas, of course. He usually came back for Thanksgiving and made a long weekend of it. The air was a bit calmer now as both Molly and Christian seemed resigned to their decisions. Molly had baked a special coffee cake to have for breakfast and Dan happily dug in to a generous piece. After they finished eating, Dan lingered for a bit, reading the paper and talking stocks with Christian. Christian had always been intrigued by what Dan did, but since he'd been staying with them, he asked questions to get a better understanding of how Dan approached the market and was interested in learning how he picked which stocks to follow. Christian was a quick learner and Dan enjoyed exchanging ideas with him.

They headed over to Molly's mother and aunt's place a little before noon, and soon after, Traci, Travis and their parents arrived. There was too much food and Molly's Aunt Betty was mixing mimosas for everyone and put Dan on champagne duty, so he was charged with opening a new bottle and pouring the proper amount of champagne into each glass. After an hour or so of socializing and snacking on nuts and various cheeses, shrimp cocktail, and dips and chips, Aunt Betty announced that dinner was served and they all gathered in the dining room where Traci's father did the honors and carved the turkey.

An hour later, after the table had been cleared and pies had been served, Molly's mother and Aunt shooed them all into the family room to relax while they finished cleaning up in the kitchen. Traci's mother, Molly, and Traci offered to help, but they insisted that they join the others. So, Dan was pleased to find himself settled next to Traci on a very comfortable sofa while they picked at pieces of pecan pie they had no room for.

"Your mother made this?" Dan asked. "It's crazy good." And it was. Even though he was full to the brim, he couldn't stop eating the pie.

"Yes, it's the one thing she loves to make and it wouldn't be Thanksgiving without her pecan pie." They sat in silence for a bit after that, watching the football game and enjoying the afternoon. Dan realized that after today there was no upcoming event where he'd see Traci. The idea of another week going by without seeing her wasn't appealing. He didn't want to wait even a day.

"What are you up to tomorrow night?" he asked her.

"Nothing. Probably just falling into bed early. It should be a crazy day."

"Right, busiest shopping day of the year. So, you'll be too tired to make dinner after that. Why don't you come by and I'll have dinner waiting for you? I'd suggest going out, but maybe you'll be too tired for that?"

"I'd love to just come over, that sounds wonderful. You sure you don't mind cooking? We can always get take-out or something?"

"What, do you doubt my cooking skills?" Dan teased. "I actually like to cook. I just don't do it that often. Prepare to be impressed."

"Just the fact that you're cooking anything and I don't have to is enough to impress me." Traci grinned at that and Dan realized that for the first time in a long time, he wasn't just tolerating a holiday, he was actually enjoying it.

"I'm here to pick up my Santa suit."

Traci turned at the sound of the familiar voice. Billy was behind her, waiting patiently for her line of customers to wind down. The store had been insanely busy as it always was on the Friday after Thanksgiving. It was starting to quiet a bit, though, as the biggest crowds always came earlier in the day. It was almost six and her co-worker, Adele, was waiting behind her with a new drawer of money. She pulled her drawer out so Adele could slip hers in and start her evening shift. Traci then hit a few buttons on the register to switch the user over to Adele.

"Billy, let me drop this in the office and I'll meet you back here with the suit."

She handed her drawer to Tom, the store manager, when she entered the back room and then went hunting for Billy's Santa outfit. It was wedged in an otherwise empty locker, clean and folded from last year. She found a plastic bag to put it in and then carried it out to Billy.

"Here you go. We'll see you about eleven tomorrow."

But Billy wasn't done yet. "What are you doing now? Want to grab a bite to eat? Catch up a bit? I haven't talked to you in ages."

"I can't, Billy. I'm beat." She hoped he'd leave it at that, but being Billy, he didn't.

"But you have to eat. Come on, my treat," he pleaded.

"I actually have prior plans," she admitted.

"A date?" A dark look crossed his face so Traci quickly decided to tell a white lie.

"No, just going over to Molly's for dinner." It wasn't totally a lie; technically she was going to where Molly lived, sort of.

"Oh, okay. Another time, then."

"See you tomorrow, Billy. Have a good night."

He left and then a few minutes later, she did, too. She'd talked briefly with Dan on her lunch break and asked what she could bring over, a bottle of wine maybe? He told her not to bring anything, that he had everything taken care of, including wine. But still, she didn't want to show up empty-handed, so she'd picked out a box of brownies from the store bakery. They were thick and fudgy and she figured they'd go well with anything.

Twenty minutes later she pulled into the ranch driveway and parked in front of Dan's door. There were no other cars there; Christian and Molly must have gone out somewhere.

Traci knocked on the front door and Dan hollered to come on in. She stepped inside and saw him feeding wood into a roaring fire. He stood up and closed the door of the wood stove. The room was cozy and warm and Traci was glad to be there. She slipped off her coat and handed the box of brownies to Dan when he came over to give her a welcome hug.

"I told you not to bring anything," he said, and then when he saw what was in the box he added, "but I'm glad you did. These look great. Let's eat."

He led her into the dining room where the table was set with twin tapered candles burning softly and he'd already poured red wine for both of them. "We're having steak, so I thought a red would be good."

"Sounds perfect," she said as she settled into her chair and placed a napkin on her lap.

"I thought we could start with salad, while the steaks rest for a few minutes. Oh, and I have bread, hold on." He ran back to the kitchen and returned a moment later with a crusty loaf and a serrated knife. He sliced a few pieces and Traci reached for one. It was still hot from the oven. She spread a bit of butter on it and took a bite.

"This is heaven." It tasted wonderful and she was feeling quite content. The wine was delicious, as well.

"You haven't tasted anything, yet. Just wait." They started on their salads and then Dan brought the steaks out a few minutes later. They were tenderloin steaks and had a bubbling crust of panko crumbs and blue cheese on top, smothered in a red wine reduction sauce. Baby spinach and a simple baked potato were on the side.

Traci cut into the steak and took a bite. "Amazing. How did you learn to cook like this?" She was more than impressed.

Dan looked pleased at the compliment. "It's not that difficult, really. This is one of the few dishes I have down pat. One of my buddies worked as a sous chef at a high end restaurant in Chicago during college. He taught me how to make this and a few other things. I'd be happy to show you sometime."

"I'd love that." The vibe between them felt different now. Traci had to admit the idea of a private cooking lesson with Dan was inviting.

"How's your leg feeling? I noticed that you weren't using the crutches just now." As happy as she was for him to be healing, she hated the idea of him going back to Chicago.

"I go see the doctor next week for a check-in. It feels stronger, but I'm also being super careful and still using the crutches when I go outside."

Traci wondered if he had a return date in mind. He'd never mentioned it. She was tempted to ask, but didn't want to dampen the mood. Instead, she said, "That's good. Probably not a good idea to rush anything."

After dinner, Traci helped Dan clear the plates and put

them in the dishwasher. Dan was ready for a brownie, but Traci was still too full, so he grabbed one and they refilled their wine glasses and then went into the family room and settled onto Dan's new, buttery soft leather sofa. He clicked on the new big screen TV and scrolled through the listings until they found a movie that looked good.

"So, tell me about your day," Dan asked while the movie started to load up. "Is Black Friday really that crazy?"

Traci laughed. "It is. We opened two hours early for the true bargain shoppers and there's always a long line waiting to get in. After that it was non-stop. I just stood at the register and barely moved all day, except to ring people in." She absent mindedly rubbed her right foot, which had started to ache a few hours ago. It didn't usually bother her on a normal day because she'd be moving around so much. But staying in the same position for hours on end killed her feet.

"Hazards of the job?" Dan had noticed her rubbing her foot.

"Not usually, just on days like this."

"Spin around and give me your foot," he ordered.

"What?" Traci was flustered for a moment.

"Seriously, I've been told I give a mean foot massage."

Traci did as she was told, turned sideways, snuggled into the many pillows on the sofa, and lifted her right foot up. Dan took hold and started pressing and kneading and it felt beyond fabulous. A soft moan escaped her and Dan chuckled.

"I take it you like that."

"Like is an understatement," Traci agreed.

"Give me your other one," he commanded after he'd had his way with her right foot. Traci happily complied.

After making all the muscles in that foot melt with his touch, Dan asked her to switch positions once again, so he could do her shoulders.

"You really don't have to," Traci protested weakly, as she turned around.

"Don't be silly, your shoulders must be feeling it, too. Anytime you're in the same position for hours on end, your muscles will get stiff."

"You are really good at this." Traci felt all the tension in her shoulders melt away as Dan's strong hands squeezed and kneaded her tight muscles. After he gave her shoulders a thorough rub down, he lightly ran his fingers along the side of her neck and she shivered at the direct touch of his skin against hers. He increased the pressure a bit and lightly pressed at the base of her head, then moved his hands up to massage her scalp. Finally, he stopped and Traci reluctantly shifted her position so that she was sitting side by side. But Dan wasn't done yet.

"There's one more spot that needs loosening up," he said with a twinkle in his eye. Traci caught her breath as Dan leaned in and lightly touched his lips against hers and then, meeting no resistance, he deepened the kiss.

Traci was feeling so relaxed that Dan's kiss initially caught her off-guard, but she quickly recovered and sank into it, enjoying the feeling of his lips against hers. He was a good kisser, and the chemistry that she'd suspected might be there between them was even better than she imagined. She didn't want the kiss to end, but finally, they came up for air and then Dan pulled her in tightly against him and they snuggled like that for the next few hours as they watched a romantic comedy with occasional breaks for kissing.

When the movie ended, she reluctantly got up to leave as she knew the next day would be almost as busy, especially with the arrival of Santa Claus.

Dan pulled her in for a good-bye kiss at the door and then said, "I'm so glad you came over. Next time I'm taking you out on a real date."

"This was plenty real enough for me." She gave him a final kiss and then headed home, thinking how the night with Dan had been just about perfect.

Chapter Twelve

*D*an usually looked forward to relaxing on a Saturday, getting things done around the house and heading out with friends or a date in the evening. But, things were a bit quieter in Beauville. He wasn't driving yet, so he wasn't out and about running errands, and there were no friends to go out with. Except for Traci, but they'd just gone out the night before and he didn't want to rush anything with her. So, that left Christian and Molly, who weren't spending much time together, as Molly was getting ready to head back to Manhattan in two days. But still, he was getting tired of his own company.

He made a quick call to the house to see what they were up to and Molly informed him that she was on her way out, off to visit with her mom and aunt, but that Christian was very much available. His brother got on the phone and suggested that they go out for burgers and beers.

Christian drove, and twenty minutes later they were sitting at the bar at Delancey's, drinking beer and eating peanuts while they waited for their burgers to arrive. Christian was quieter than usual and Dan knew he wasn't happy about Molly leaving. Yet, he also knew that his brother was too stubborn to do anything about it.

They chatted about nothing in particular until their food arrived, and then as soon as Dan had taken his first bite of his oversized Burger, Christian asked him, "So, what is going on with you and Traci? Noticed her car was here awfully late last night."

Dan swallowed and took his time answering. His brother had made it more than clear that he didn't think it was a good idea for him to get involved with Traci.

"I enjoy her company," he said simply. Which was true. She was his favorite person to spend time with in Beauville. Christian left it at that and they continued eating in comfortable silence until their burgers were gone. Ted, the bartender, came by, cleared their plates away and asked them if they wanted another beer. They both said yes at the same time and a moment later had a fresh beer in front of them. The bar was getting full as there were college football games going on several channels. Dan had thought that getting out on a Saturday night might cheer Christian up and get his mind off Molly leaving, but it actually seemed to have the opposite effect. They spent several hours there and Christian seemed more and more down as the night went on. Finally, Dan couldn't take it anymore. He hadn't said much to his brother thus far, figuring his relationship with Molly was his business and he didn't need Dan butting in. But this moping around before she'd even left was ridiculous.

"Why don't you just ask her to stay?" he asked. But Christian was focused intently on the game playing on the closest TV, and didn't respond. So, he asked the question again.

"I heard you the first time," Christian said as he took another sip of beer and kept his eyes on the TV.

"Okay, then. So?"

"So, what? I can't ask her to stay now. It's too late for that. Even if I wanted to. Decisions have been made. People are expecting her."

Dan said nothing to that. What could he say?

"Wouldn't be right," Christian added and shifted his gaze to Dan.

"I suppose not," Dan said, but wasn't sure if he really agreed with his brother.

"I'll be fine. I'm sure she will, too. She's getting everything she always wanted." Christian's voice was sad.

"Not everything," Dan reminded him.

Christian was silent for a moment, then turned his attention back to the game and said, "So, if you were going to bet, who would you pick?"

"I have no idea."

Traci wasn't used to working on Sundays. Though Snow's was open every Sunday, from eleven a.m. to six p.m., she usually had Sunday and Monday off. But, not during the Christmas season. Their store was very busy, even on Sundays, and Traci loved the energy of it all. People seemed to have caught the Christmas spirit by this time and the kids loved seeing Santa and sitting on his lap.

Though Santa wasn't where he should be. The picture-taking officially started at 11:30 a.m., but Billy was always in his chair by eleven a.m., talking and joking with everyone. Kids loved it, and having a jovial Santa drew them over to the area. By 11:30, there was always a small line, which grew longer and stayed constant as the day progressed. Traci grew concerned when 11:10 approached and there was still no Billy. It wasn't like him to be late.

Five minutes later, as she was busy ringing in a customer's order, she caught a glimpse of Billy coming in the front door, and relaxed. She didn't have a back-up plan in place in case Billy was sick. Plus, they were just too busy this time of year and everyone was needed on the floor. She hadn't given it much thought because she knew Billy so well and knew he could be counted on. He'd always been so reliable.

A few minutes later, Traci saw Billy climbing into his Santa chair and noticed that he looked a bit unsteady. She finished ringing up the two customers that were waiting, and told Adele, who was also working the registers in her department, that she'd be right back. Traci walked towards Billy with a sense of dread.

She was ten feet away from him when the smell of alcohol washed over her. It seemed to be emanating from his pores and Traci was shocked. How could Billy be drunk this early in the day? His eyes were glassy and he had a silly smile on his face. Fortunately, no one else was in the immediate area yet.

"Good morning, beautiful." His tone was painful, the words slow and slurred. Traci thought fast. She had to get him out of there immediately, before any children or parents realized what kind of a state he was in. She also needed to line-up a Santa, asap. But who could she call? Her brother was the first one she thought of, but Travis was out of town for the weekend. Then she thought of Dan, but dismissed that idea immediately. How could she ask someone who hated the holidays so much to play Santa? She got her phone out of her pocket quickly and texted Adele that she would be right back, then glanced her way to make sure she got the message. Adele looked over and waved and Traci moved into react mode.

"Billy, could you come with me please, I need to show you something."

"Sure thing I'll follow you anywhere, you know that." Billy was in a happy, silly mood, thankfully. Sometimes the alcohol did that to him, but his mood could shift in a second. Traci needed to get him out of the store as fast as possible.

Billy followed her out back and they walked past Gerry, the assistant store manager, who was on the phone in the back office.

"Everything okay?" he asked as Billy walked unsteadily behind him.

"Billy's not feeling well," Traci said. "I'm going to run him home, will be right back."

"Do you have another Santa coming?"

"I think so. I have someone I'm going to call."

"Good." Gerry turned his attention back to the call and Traci led Billy out the back door to her car.

"What are we doing?" Billy looked confused, and now that they were outside of the store, Traci felt her irritation simmer to the surface.

"Get in Billy, I'm taking you home." She opened her door and was about to get in, but Billy wasn't moving. He stood still, obviously trying to process what was happening.

"But I just got here. I'm supposed to be Santa."

"Yes, you are, but that's not going to happen today. Not in the condition you're in. You're drunk, Billy."

"I'm not drunk. I haven't had a thing to drink today."

"Nothing? I find that hard to believe."

"I swear it. I did have maybe have a few too many last night, though, and my back was killing me this morning, probably from sitting in that chair all day yesterday. Not that I mind. I love playing Santa."

"I know you do." Traci's irritation lessened a bit. She believed that Billy hadn't been drinking that morning, but he must have still had enough in his system when he woke up that he was affected much more than usual when he took his pain meds.

"My back feels much better now," he added.

Traci chuckled. "I'm sure it does. Get in the car Billy. I need to take you home. You can't do this today."

"Okay." Billy looked resigned as he opened the door on his side and got in.

He lived just five minutes down the road in a small ranch

house. Traci pulled into the driveway and said, "We need the suit, Billy."

"Right. I'll be back in a minute." He shuffled to the front door, which fortunately wasn't locked, and went in. While she was waiting, Traci got out her phone and called Dan. Though he was about the least appropriate person for the job, he was her only option at such short notice. He still didn't drive, because of his leg, so she was fairly certain that he was available. He picked up on the first ring, "Well, this is a nice surprise. How are you?"

"Hi, Dan. I've been better. I'm actually calling with a favor to ask of you." She explained the situation and Dan was silent for a moment and then he chuckled.

"Sure, I'll help you out. It's really kind of comical when you think about it. Me, of all people, playing Santa."

"Thanks a million! You're a life-saver. I'm dropping off Billy now and will swing by in a few minutes to get you." Dan agreed and Traci hung up and looked at the clock. It had been almost five minutes now. What was Billy doing? She got out of the car and walked up to the front door and knocked. Then she knocked harder. Still nothing. She pushed open the door and stepped in. Billy was sprawled across the sofa. The top half of his Santa suit was strewn on the floor. His bright red pants were still on him as he lay there snoring loudly. Traci sighed, then realized that there was really no need to wake him. The Santa pants were one size fits all and had an elastic waist, so she walked over, slipped off his shoes and pulled hard on the pants. After a moment, they came loose and slid off easily. Traci gathered the outfit and left Billy asleep on the sofa. She had a feeling that when he woke up from this, he'd be feeling less than jovial. Once this wore off, he'd likely be feeling pretty miserable. She was glad that she wouldn't be around to see it.

Fifteen minutes later, Traci was back at Snow's with Dan. He hardly needed to use the crutches now, but had them along just in case. Traci showed him where the men's locker room was so he could change into his Santa suit. A few minutes later, he reappeared and looked pretty good, for a last minute Santa. She led him over to his area, where there was already a long line of impatient families waiting.

"So, what exactly do I do?" he asked.

"It's easy. Just sit in the chair and ask each kid what they want for Christmas."

"That's it?" He seemed surprised.

"That's it. Just smile for the camera and try to have fun."

Chapter Thirteen

J ust try to have fun..." Dan briefly thought of what Traci said as he settled into the Santa chair and prepared for the day ahead. Playing Santa, in public, was about as surreal as it could possibly get. When Traci had called him earlier and asked him to fill in as the store Santa, his immediate first reaction was a resounding "no way", and he was about to say so, but something in her voice made him pause. Traci was desperate, and she knew how he felt about the holidays. For her to have called and asked him, of all people, meant that she was really stuck. Given the timing, he also knew that there was a line of kids likely waiting to see Santa and that was impossible to say no to. Dan wasn't a fan of the holidays, but he wasn't exactly a Scrooge; not yet, anyway. Though admittedly, in recent years, he'd been feeling more and more like one.

The first child, a boy of about six, made his way eagerly towards him and Dan helped the boy onto his lap. He drew a blank for a moment with all the many eyes upon him and then remembered what he was supposed to say.

"What's your name, young man?" he asked in a somewhat deeper voice than usual.

"Tommy. Are you Santa?" His voice was full of hope, and wonder.

"Yes, Tommy, I'm Santa. Have you been a good boy this year?"

"Yes, except for last week when I got in trouble in school." He looked sad for a moment and then explained. "Teacher said I was talking in class too much. I guess I was."

Dan tried not to chuckle, as he could certainly relate. "Tommy, you know what? Don't tell anyone, but I used to do that, too. I just couldn't help it sometimes."

Tommy's face lit up and a smile stretched across his face. Dan glanced at Jim, the young man manning the camera at that moment, sensing it was ideal for a picture. Jim nodded and the flash went off. Dan then asked his final question. "So, Tommy, what would you like Santa to bring you this year?"

"Santa, I really, really, really want a bike of my own. I've been practicing on my cousin Harrison's and I want one just like his."

"Okay, Tommy, we'll see what we can do. Merry Christmas!" Dan looked up and caught the eye of Tommy's mother who came forward to take his hand as he slid off Dan's lap.

"Bye, Santa!" Tommy walked off, waving and happy as the next child was nudged forward.

By six o'clock, the store was officially closed and Dan was exhausted and starving. He'd worked straight through without a break even though Traci had stopped by and suggested he grab a quick bite to eat. He wasn't hungry then, though, and didn't want to disappoint the line of wide-eyed children who'd been waiting so patiently to see Santa.

Surprisingly he'd actually enjoyed playing the part of Santa and the day had flown by. Dan had always had a soft spot for kids and he had to admit, if only to himself, that their excitement and wonder to see Santa was a bit contagious. Their requests were amusing, too, and ran the gamut from something as simple as a new miniature toy car to as extravagant as a ride in the space shuttle. Dan had explained to that child that space shuttle rides had been discontinued, and did he have a second choice? He did, one that was much more reasonable, a toy of some sort, so that was good.

He changed quickly, and left the Santa suit in an empty bin where Traci had indicated so that it would be sent out for cleaning during the week and ready for the next shift.

Traci was waiting for him when he emerged in his regular clothes and they headed out to her car.

"I can't thank you enough," she said.

"It was no big deal, I really didn't mind at all."

"That's good to know. Billy should be fine, I hope, for next weekend, but just in case, would you be up for filling in again?"

Dan didn't even have to think about it this time. "Sure, just let me know. It's not like my social calendar is over-flowing these days."

Traci smiled at that. "Well, if you don't have dinner plans tonight, I'd love to treat you to pizza at my place, as a thank you."

"Pizza sounds perfect." Dan's stomach rumbled in agreement and they both laughed.

"You must be starving. Why don't you call ahead and order for us? I have the number saved in my phone."

"What do you want on your pizza?"

"I like almost anything except anchovies."

"Sausage, peppers and onions sound good?" Dan asked.

"Sounds great."

Dan called to place the order and soon after, they arrived at Traci's condo. They went in and Traci offered him a beer, which he happily accepted, and she poured herself a glass of red wine and they both collapsed on her oversized sofa and clicked on the TV. They chatted easily as they waited for the pizza. Fortunately, they didn't have to wait too long. As soon as it arrived, Traci insisted on paying, and then they dove in. Dan was starting on his fourth slice as Traci was finishing her second when there was a knock on the door. Traci froze and had a bit of a panicked look on her face.

"Are you expecting someone?" Dan asked.

"No, and there's only one person that usually drops by unannounced." She got up and slowly opened the door. Billy was standing outside and didn't see Dan, at first.

"Hey Traci, just wanted to stop by to apologize for this morning. I hope that I didn't screw things up too badly for you."

"We found someone to fill in," Traci said and then added, "I hope you're feeling better?"

"Sort of, I've been fighting the hangover from hell all day. Back's been acting up, too. Can I come in?"

"I don't think that's a good idea, Billy."

"Why not? You got company or something?" Dan picked up a belligerent tone in Billy's voice that made him sit up and pay closer attention.

"Billy, I'm actually in the middle of dinner right now."

Billy leaned in to get a look inside and saw Dan sitting on the sofa.

"So, are you two dating now?" His tone was loud and accusatory and Traci glanced over at Dan, with an apologetic look. He stood up and walked over towards her, so they were both facing Billy together.

"Dan was nice enough to fill in for you today, and now we're having a bite to eat. We're going to get back to our pizza now."

That was Billy's cue to leave, but it didn't seem to register. He stood glaring at the two of them until it got awkward.

"Good night, Billy." Dan said.

"Are you trying to get rid of me? So you can get back to your date? I knew the two of you were dating when I saw you at Isabella's."

"Billy, this is ridiculous. Who I do or don't date is none of your business."

"We're engaged!" Billy yelled.

"Billy, I gave you back the ring. We're not engaged."

"You were cheating on me with him! That's why you were always out at the ranch." Billy lunged forward and looked like he intended to swing at Dan, but his foot caught on the front step and he fell forward instead, and his balance was off. He tumbled into the room and fell awkwardly. When he tried to get up and then fell back down, Traci pulled out her cell phone and punched in a number. A moment later Dan heard her say, "Mr. Sears? This is Traci. Billy stopped by unexpectedly and I think it would be a good idea if you came and brought him home." She was silent for a moment and then said, in a much quieter voice, "Yes, it does seem like he has been having some of those kinds of issues lately."

Billy was still sitting on the floor, glaring at both of them. Traci ended the call and then told him that his father was on his way. Billy said nothing to that. Keeping an eye on him, they both sat back down and started eating their pizza again. Traci offered Billy a slice, which he declined.

"I don't want your pizza." He sat there sulking for the next five minutes while they ate in an uncomfortable silence.

A knock on the door announced the arrival of Billy's father and older brother, Jim, who came in and helped Billy up. While his brother led him out to the car, Billy's father pulled Traci aside and they went into the kitchen for a minute then came back out.

"I'm sorry we are seeing you again under these circumstances. We're going to get some help for Billy." His tone was apologetic and concerned. As soon as they left, Traci filled Dan in on their conversation in the kitchen.

"The family has been concerned about Billy for a while. I told his father about the state he was in this morning and that he wasn't able to be Santa. He said they'd talked about what they might need to do if things got worse and it's seems like it might be time now for Billy to go away and get some help; to go into a treatment center and get the pain meds and drinking under control."

"Is he an alcoholic?" Dan asked.

"I honestly don't know. I never thought so. He was just a social drinker. Sometimes he'd have one or two, other times a few more, but it never got out of control until he started taking the pain meds for his back."

"I'm glad you ended things with him. He seems like a bit of a loose cannon."

Traci was quiet for a moment and then sighed. "Billy's really a great guy, when he's not drinking or on the pain meds, but both have really changed him this past year. He's not the same person and I didn't like the direction that things were heading. I hope he can get help and get back on track."

They finished the rest of their pizza and when Traci caught him yawning for the third time, she insisted on driving him home. Dan would have loved to stay longer, but he knew they were both tired and he didn't want her to be out too late driving him around. He couldn't wait until the doctor cleared him to drive. His next check-in was only a week away and he was hoping he might get the okay, then.

"Do you have any plans Thursday night?" he asked as she pulled into his driveway.

Traci thought for a moment. "Just rehearsal for the holiday pageant, but that ends around seven. I'm free after that."

"Okay, great. I'll call you during the day then and we'll make a plan."

Dan gave Traci a quick kiss goodbye and then watched as her car drove away. His plan, if all went well, was to get the okay to drive on Thursday and surprise Traci by coming to pick her up.

***

Traci stopped by her house after work and had about ten minutes to freshen up before she had to run out again to be to the church by 5:30 for pageant practice. The outfit she had on was fine for Snow's but it wasn't anything special, and since she was meeting up with Dan for dinner, she wanted to look nice. She pulled off the perfectly fine tan sweater and slipped into a soft, rosy pink cashmere one instead. Instantly, she felt her mood lift. A quick brush of her hair and a bit of lipstick and she was off.

As she drove to the church, she thought back to her call earlier in the day. Molly had called on her lunch break to say hello and they chatted for almost a half-hour. She sounded a bit down and Traci knew she was missing Christian, so she was surprised when Molly admitted that she had a date of sorts lined up. Molly was even less ready for a new relationship than Traci was, and yet she was getting out and meeting people. Maybe it wasn't too soon for her to start dating again, too. Her head told her that Dan wasn't a good candidate. He was used to running in a different crowd and he'd made it very clear that his stay here was temporary and that as soon as he possibly could, he'd be heading back to Chicago and to his life there.

But, he wasn't going anywhere for at least another month or two. So why not enjoy his company while he was here? She'd just have to make sure to keep things light and casual.

At least the stress of Billy was finally gone. His father had called earlier as well, to give her the update that Billy had agreed to go away to a treatment center for a month. Traci was glad to hear that the school was fully supportive and put him on a leave of absence. Her heart went out to him; she hoped that he could get himself back on track.

When she arrived at church, Molly's mom and Aunt Betty were inside, putting out snacks for the kids to have after rehearsal and making coffee for the adults to have right away. They were also both helping with the costumes for the children. Aunt Betty had a real talent for sewing, which came in handy for these productions.

Once the rest of the children arrived, Traci got everyone into place in the sanctuary. There was a large open area that was a few steps up and made for a perfect stage. They were also fortunate to have the musical director and a small team of six musicians who were doing the run through today, too. They were bringing the nativity scene to life, with Mary and Joseph looking for shelter and the wise men coming to offer their gifts. Traci was so intent on what she was doing, directing the children here and there and reminding them of their lines when necessary that she didn't even notice when Dan quietly walked in.

❧✻❧

Dan hadn't stepped foot in a church in many years. His family had never been big church-goers. Like many people, they went twice a year- on the Christmas and Easter plan, as his Dad used to say. They usually went to one of the earlier services on Christmas Eve, so they would be home in plenty of time to begin welcoming guests to their holiday open house. Dan had never minded going, but once his parents died on Christmas Eve, it had never really crossed his mind to go again. That wasn't entirely true; he had considered it, the first year after they were gone, but he just as quickly dismissed the idea and never revisited it again. It was easier to just distance himself from anything overly festive or holiday related, which is why he was still a bit surprised by how much he'd enjoyed playing Santa for Traci. But then he told himself it was really the idea of helping Traci that he liked.

When he walked into the church, he heard the music and the lights and saw Traci down front, directing the rehearsal. He walked as softly as he could and sat down off to the side, where he wouldn't be a distraction. He was a few minutes early. Traci had told him to come around seven, and as he'd hoped, he was given the thumbs up to drive again at his doctor's appointment. Christian had taken the time to drive him there and Dan didn't want to keep him from work any longer than necessary, so even though he offered to swing by the car rental place, Dan knew that would probably take a while, so he told him to just drop him off and he'd take care of it himself. He called and arranged for a short-term lease from the local car rental agency and they'd dropped it off about an hour ago. He couldn't wait to take it out for a spin and was looking forward to finally taking Traci out on a proper date.

There was no one else in the audience, except for him, and after a few minutes, he found himself caught up in the familiar story and simple sweetness of the program the children were doing. As most people did, he knew the stories by heart and the music they were playing created the perfect mood of hope and joy. The program ended with the children singing the classic Christmas carol *Silent Night* and the accompanying music was haunting and beautiful. Dan was surprised when a sudden feeling of peace and quiet joy swept over him. It took him by surprise.

When the music stopped and the room was silent, Dan impulsively stood up and clapped. The children turned at the sound and several started giggling. The mood quickly shifted back to normal and all the children began talking at once and running around, while the adults started to move chairs and things back to the way they had been. Traci walked over to him and smiled. "Thanks for the applause. The kids really did a great job."

"I was clapping for you, too," Dan said. "Are you ready to head out?"

"In a few minutes. I just need to help straighten things out."

"I can help, too; just show me what to do."

Traci led him over to where they were moving chairs back to where they were supposed to be. Within minutes, everything was in order. Molly's mom and Aunt Betty were getting ready to head out, too.

"Have you talked to Molly lately?" Aunt Betty asked as they all walked out to the parking lot.

"She called earlier today, actually, and we caught up. It sounds like she's doing well."

"Did she mention that she has a date lined up? With an

architect!" Aunt Betty seemed particularly impressed by that and Dan wondered how Christian would feel about this particular bit of gossip.

"She did, actually. He's a friend of someone she works with I think."

"Sounds they really hit it off, going on their second date this weekend." Aunt Betty's excitement was cut off by Molly's mom who said, "It's just a date. Don't make it into more than it is."

"Well, we're off. Have a good night," Traci said as they got closer to their cars.

"Do you want to drop your car off at your house and then we can head out?" Dan asked.

"You got the okay to drive? That's great! I'm sorry, I forgot you had your appointment today."

"Yeah, saw the Doc this afternoon. I went out immediately and rented a car. It's right over there, the blue one." It was a blue Volvo sedan. After the accident he'd had, all Dan really cared about was that he had a solid, safe car. The agent he spoke with recommended the Volvo, so he went with it.

"Very nice! I bet it felt good to drive again?"

"Yeah, it kind of feels like I have my freedom back a little," Dan admitted."I really missed driving."

He followed Traci back to her house and then they went off to dinner and movie. As always, Dan loved being with Traci and they had a great time at Eduardo's, the small local restaurant that was Traci's favorite. It wasn't as busy or as fancy as Delancey's, but the food was fresh and the atmosphere was cozy, with candles glowing softly on all the tables. After the movie, Dan drove back to Traci's place and walked her to the door. It wasn't too late, so he was happy to accept her offer of coffee.

Traci made them each a cup and they settled on her comfy sofa.

"I had a great time tonight," Dan said.

"I did, too. I've really enjoyed spending time with you." A cloud passed over Traci's face for a brief moment.

"What is it?"

"Nothing, I'm just not looking forward to you leaving, and I know the time is coming soon."

"I know. I'll probably be able to head back in a few weeks, as soon as I finish up the physical therapy. Right after the New Year."

"That's about what I figured."

" Have you ever been to Chicago?" He'd love to show her around his favorite city.

"No, never."

"Well, you'll have to come visit. I'll play tourist with you."

Traci smiled, though her eyes still looked a bit sad. "That sounds fun."

"I'm serious. I really want you to come visit. I don't want what we have to stop when I go home to Chicago. I really like you."

Traci smiled at that and put her hand on top of his. "Me, too."

Dan leaned over then and pulled Traci close to him. His lips found hers and they kissed. She melted into him and he deepened the kiss. Just as he was ready to take things to the next level, Traci pulled back.

"I love spending time with you, but I need to take this

part of things slow. It's just too soon for me. I didn't think things would ever get to this point with us."

"What do you mean?" Dan's mind was still on kissing Traci, and what she was saying wasn't sinking in.

"I've really enjoyed spending time with you and it's been nice, comfortable really, because there was no pressure. I didn't have to worry about it going anywhere because you were going to be heading back soon. I guess I just didn't think this far ahead, to what would happen if you wanted to keep dating. It sounds silly, I know, but after all the drama with Billy, it was nice to just be with you."

"Oh, okay. It's totally okay. You need more time. I get that." Dan was disappointed, but he did understand. Clearly, Traci wasn't over Billy yet.

"You don't mind, really? That's a relief." Traci seemed a little nervous, confused even.

"We'll just take things slow, as slow as you need to go. Sound good?"

Traci leaned in and gave him a quick, soft kiss. "Sounds wonderful. Thank you."

Dan stood up and Traci walked him to the door and they kissed again.

"Want to come by after work tomorrow? We can make it a movie night?"

"Sure, that sounds great. Fridays have been insane at the store lately. A night in sounds perfect."

Chapter Fourteen

Traci met her best friend, Jennifer, at the Morning Muffin the next day before work. Jen had been away for the past two months on a research trip to Scotland and Ireland. Though born and brought up in Beauville, Jen made a very good living as a romance writer. Her books topped the historical romance charts and since she could write anywhere, loved to travel, and was, as she put it, "totally single", Jen often took the opportunity to research and write her books in exotic settings. She'd completely written the first draft of her latest book overseas, spending a month in each country, and was now home, getting ready to edit and then publish what was sure to be her next bestseller..

So, though they'd kept up by email, Traci hadn't shared that she was starting to really fall for Dan. But, it took Jen all of about ten minutes to figure it out.

"You love him!" she announced, and Traci felt her cheeks blush. Jen was like that. She wasn't your typical quiet and reserved writer. She was outgoing and charismatic, exuding energy and a sense of fun that drew people to her. She was always the life of the party and admittedly enjoyed the attention. She was definitely fun to be around and Traci had missed her.

"I don't know about that. I do like him a lot, and I really missed you."

"I missed you like crazy, too, but from what I see and hear, you're more in love with this Dan than you ever were with Billy. I never did like the two of you together, you know." She took a big bite of her cheese danish while Traci smiled. Jen had never hesitated to share her opinion and she'd been thrilled to hear that Traci had, as she put it, "finally dumped him."

"I do really like Dan, but I'm just a little unsure. We're very different and he has a life in Chicago. I'm just not sure I'd fit in." That was her biggest fear; that Dan was interested now, here in Beauville where he really didn't know anyone, but what about when he was back in Chicago and around the group of friends that lived a very different lifestyle than she was used to? Would he still be interested then? Or would she suddenly seem dull, and boring? More than anything, she was afraid of letting herself go, of really falling for him, and then having her heart broken.

"Oh, don't be ridiculous! You're fabulous! Of course you'll fit in. His friends will love you." Traci loved that about Jen; she was such a good friend and was always so positive.

"I don't know. I hope so," Traci said.

"So, when will I meet him? We need to go out and celebrate. I know, I'll have a party! That will be a good excuse to get Isabella out, too. She's been doing nothing but working since she and Christian split up." Isabella was Jen's older sister and they were very close, but Traci had never spent much time around Isabella and didn't feel like she knew her very well. Truth be told, she was so glamorous and successful that Traci found her a bit intimidating. Jen had once explained that Isabella was more of a guy's girl; aside from Jen, she didn't have many female friends.

"A party sounds fun," Traci said. She wasn't much of a big party person, though; she tended to prefer smaller gatherings. Jen didn't do small, though, so Traci knew half the town was likely to be there. Dan would probably love it. He and Jen were similar that way. They were so isolated with their work that they both loved to get out and mingle.

"Okay, I'll start planning it. Let's do it this Saturday."

"This Saturday, as in tomorrow?" Traci couldn't imagine whipping a party up in a day, but for Jen it was just a matter of calling everyone she knew, telling them she was back in town and that they should come over for a 'get-together'. It always grew into a blow-out party. Traci had to admit, Jen's parties were always a good time.

"Yes, absolutely tomorrow. I can't wait!"

Dan was sitting at his desk, intently focused on one of his two monitors, when his phone rang. An emerging pattern was starting to take shape on one of his most volatile stocks and it needed his full attention. He ignored the phone and, eventually, it stopped ringing and then a ding informed him that whoever it was had left a voice message. He could deal with it later. A few minutes later his phone beeped again, this time announcing a text message. He reached for his phone, saw it was from his best friend Jeff's kid sister, Suzanne, and read, "Do you miss me?" at which he smiled. Suzanne was always so dramatic but she was a good friend. "Desperately," he quickly texted back and then turned his attention back to the monitor. A few seconds later, his phone pinged again and Suzanne replied, "Good, talk soon!" That was so Suzanne; he hadn't heard from her in weeks. He turned his focus back to his stocks and didn't stop again until hours later when the market closed. It was a few minutes past six when his phone rang again and he expected it to be Traci, but instead was surprised to see Suzanne's number on the Caller ID.

"Hey, Suzanne, what are you up to?"

"I'm pulling into your driveway, actually. I think this is the right place, anyway. You really are out in the middle of nowhere!"

"What! You're here? Are you serious?" Dan got up and walked over to the window and sure enough, a black Range Rover was heading towards the house. It had to be her; no one else he knew around here drove a car like that.

"Didn't you get my message earlier? I called to tell you I was about to get on a plane and head out to see you. You did say I could come visit anytime."

Dan had completely forgotten about the call earlier and hadn't listened to the voice mail. "Right, of course I did. I just can't believe you're here. How come you didn't call sooner?"

"Well, it was kind of last minute and I thought it would be fun to surprise you. You're surprised, right?"

"Yeah, you could say that."

"But, it's a good surprise I hope? I'm just here for a few days. I won't get in your way, I promise. I just needed to get away, and we always have so much fun together." Her voice was bubbly and excited and her enthusiasm was as contagious as always.

"No, it's fine. I'm glad you're here. I'll be right out. Hang on." Dan hung up the phone and threw his coat on and went out to greet his unexpected guest.

Suzanne parked and got out of the car. Then she ran over to Dan and gave him a big hug and quick kiss on the lips. There wasn't anything unusual about that. Suzanne and pretty much everyone in his social group greeted each other that way, but for the first time it hit Dan kind of funny, and even though it was perfectly innocent and just Suzanne being Suzanne, Dan felt a bit guilty wondering what Traci would have thought. Traci was also due to be over shortly. How on earth would he explain Suzanne? People in Traci's circle, normal people, didn't just show up unannounced on the other side of the country like this.

"Nice car," he commented.

"It's okay. I thought it might be more practical than my usual Mercedes. You know, because of the four-wheel drive. In case of mountains."

"Right." Only Suzanne would consider a Range Rover a 'practical' car. She and Jeff each had trust funds that were so enormous that neither would ever have to work. Jeff did work, though. He and a few buddies ran a hedge fund which contributed many more millions each year to his already impressive bank account. Suzanne didn't have a steady job, but occasionally tried her hand at various ventures like painting, acting, designing shoes; it changed all the time. She was also very active with several prominent charities and so far, that seemed to be where she was most successful, helping to plan large events and making sure that all of her friends attended. She kept their social calendars full.

"I didn't bring much, just a few bags," she said as she opened the back of the car, and grabbed a small shoulder carryon and a garment bag which, by the looks of it, probably held a cocktail dress or two. As if there was any occasion in Beauville to wear a cocktail dress. Dan smiled in amusement.

"Can you grab the big one for me?" she asked as she started walking toward the door.

"Sure thing." Big was an understatement. The suitcase in the backseat was the largest he'd ever seen and it was bulging.

"How long did you say you were staying again?" he asked as he grabbed the suitcase and then they headed inside.

Chapter Fifteen

*I*t had been great to catch up earlier that morning with Jen who, as usual, was a whirlwind. Traci was excited for her to meet Dan. She had a feeling she would like him, and valued her opinion. They had been friends since the second grade and Traci always missed her when she was off on one of her extended trips. She hoped that she'd be back for a while now, but Jen had sounded more excited than usual as she'd told her about her time in Ireland, in particular, and said she might need to go back to visit some more castles there for her next book. She had a faraway look in her eyes as she spoke and Traci wondered if she might have met someone special during her time there. But, when she asked the question, Jen had just said that she'd met lots of great people but had been too busy to date anyone. She did admit, though, that she loved listening to the Irish accents and that some of the men she'd met there had been unusually charming.

The day flew by as they usually did during the holiday season, and just as Traci was getting ready to leave, she noticed Paul, one of the store managers, putting some new merchandise out and walked over to take a closer look. He was unpacking the most adorable two feet tall, fully decorated, fake Christmas trees. They even had a string of mini colored lights on them.

"Guarantee these are going to fly off the shelves. They're perfect for people who have small spaces, or who don't want to fully commit to Christmas." That got her attention.

"I'll take one," she said impulsively.

"See, I knew it!"

Traci paid for the small tree, placed it in the back seat of her car and then started driving to Dan's. She hoped that the tree wasn't a mistake, but as soon as she'd heard Paul say it would be good for people who don't want to fully commit to Christmas, she felt like she had to get it for him. She'd had her own very real tree up since the day after Thanksgiving. Her brother, Travis, had gone with her to pick it out, like he did every year, and then helped her get it home and into its stand. She loved the cheery look of the tree and secretly wished it could stay up all year. She was always sad to take it down as it felt like she was removing so much light and energy from the room. This little tree would be the perfect touch for Dan's place. It would add a hint of holiday festiveness without being over the top. And maybe it would help him feel better about the holidays in general. Or maybe he'd hate it. She hoped that wasn't the case, though.

When she pulled into the driveway, she noticed a strange car parked next to Dan's and wondered who was visiting.

Dan hadn't mentioned having anyone else over. She didn't recall ever seeing a Range Rover in Beauville, now that she thought of it. It was a beautiful car, though.

She grabbed the little tree out of the car and then knocked on the door. A moment later, it opened and Dan was standing there and behind him, a glass of wine in her hands, was a very beautiful younger woman with shiny long blonde hair and a perfect figure. She was wearing sleek, leather cowboy boots that didn't look like they'd ever seen real dirt, and jeans from a designer that Traci had never even heard of, but by the way they looked and fit, she knew they had to be very high end. Strangest of all, this woman seemed very comfortable in Dan's home. Traci started to feel a bit flustered, as if she'd interrupted something, but that didn't make any sense.

"What have you got there?" Dan asked.

"Oh, it's for you. These just came in today and I thought it would be perfect for your place. It will brighten things up, and is so small that it won't be too Christmassy."

"You're doing Christmas?" Suzanne said in surprise. "And having a tree? Who are you and what have you done with the Dan I know?" She laughed and Dan glanced at Traci with an apologetic look on his face.

"I still don't do Christmas!" Dan snapped. But Traci wasn't sure if it was directed at her or Suzanne. She took a step backwards feeling very unsure about the situation and regretting that she'd decided to bring the tree.

"It's okay, you don't have to take it. This was a bad idea. I'll just take it home." Traci fought the urge to run out and stayed put instead, waiting for a response.

"No, it's fine, really. It's very thoughtful of you." Dan

looked a little stressed as he took the tree from her hands and set it on a counter by a window.

"Aren't you going to plug it in?" Suzanne asked, clearly amused by it all. She stood up and walked over to Traci and held out her hand. "I'm Suzanne, a friend of Dan's from Chicago."

Traci shook her hand and before she could say anything, Dan spoke quickly, "Traci, this is Suzanne. She's the younger sister of my best friend Jeff. They both live near me in Chicago. Suzanne, this is Traci." He plugged the tree in and it glowed merrily.

"It's nice to meet you," Traci said politely. She wondered why Dan hadn't mentioned that Suzanne was coming to town.

"Did you two have plans tonight?" Suzanne glanced back and forth at the two of them. "Go ahead and go out, I'm beat from traveling all day, anyway."

"We were just going to stay in tonight anyway, maybe have some takeout delivered and watch a movie," Dan said.

"Oh, okay. Well, that will be fun. Traci needs a glass of wine then, don't you think?"

Yes, Traci most definitely did need a glass of wine.

"Of course, hold on." Dan went to the kitchen, got down another wine glass and filled it with the red wine that he and Suzanne were already drinking.

"We just poured this a minute or two before you got here. I brought the bottle with me to celebrate."

"Oh, what are we celebrating?" Traci asked as Dan handed her a glass of wine.

"Me being here, of course! Cheers!" Suzanne held her

glass out towards them. They all tapped glasses and then Traci took a small sip, not sure what kind of wine it was. She immediately took another, slower sip, wanting to savor the flavor. It was by far the best wine she'd ever had, full and rich and luxurious.

"This is wonderful. What is it?" Traci asked.

"It is good, isn't it? It's from my father's private collection. I was over for dinner last night and we shared a bottle. It was so amazing that I told him I had to bring one out here. It's a bordeaux from Chateau Margeaux. Daddy loves his French wines."

Traci knew just enough about wine to recognize the name and that this wine probably cost more per sip than she usually spent on a bottle. She gripped the stem of the glass a bit tighter, not wanting to risk losing a single drop.

They settled around the island in the kitchen, sipping wine and chatting while they passed around several takeout menus and finally settled on pizza again. The only other real option was Chinese and that wouldn't go at all with a stellar red wine. Pizza didn't really do it justice either, but at least there was tomato and cheese and they decided to add sliced meatballs as well.

"Where's Christian?" Suzanne asked. "I want to meet your brother, I've heard so much about him."

"He's not here. He actually took a flight to New York City this morning." Dan grinned at Traci and added, "He went to see Molly."

"He did? Did you have anything to do with that?"

"I may have passed along a bit of gossip I overheard, about a second date with an architect."

Traci chuckled at that. "Oh, good. I hope they can work things out."

Suzanne decided to change the subject, to herself.

"So, you have to come to my birthday party this year!" she exclaimed, and lightly touched Dan's arm for emphasis. Traci couldn't help but wonder if there had ever been anything between the two of them. Suzanne was so comfortable with him, maybe a little too comfortable.

Dan laughed. "I've gone to your birthday party every year. If I'm back by then, I'll definitely come."

"When is your birthday?" Traci was curious about why someone would hold a party for themselves every year.

"New Year's Eve! It's not just for me, of course; it's usually a charity event, but this year it's going to be really over the top. You only turn thirty once, right?"

"Right." New Year's Eve. That was only a little over a month away. Was Dan thinking he'd be home by then? Traci knew the time was coming, but it was too soon for her liking.

"So, Suzanne, what happened that you needed to get away so badly?" Dan asked.

Suzanne frowned for a moment, then paused to top off all their glasses.

"Dylan and I broke up." Her tone was flat.

"Oh. Jeez, I'm sorry."

"We'd been dating for almost three years," Suzanne explained to Traci. "I actually thought we might get engaged on my birthday. It would have been the perfect time to do it. But when I smelled perfume on Dylan and a few days later happened to see a disturbing text message come through from his secretary, I knew something was going on. When I confronted him, he actually seemed relieved. I don't think he had the balls to end things himself. Said he's falling for Leah... his secretary."

"That stinks. I'm sorry to hear it," Traci said.

"It's fine. It's more annoying than anything else, you know? I was really looking forward to planning the wedding. It would have been awesome."

"Were things not going well with you two?" Traci asked. Suzanne didn't seem overly broken up about the relationship ending.

"Well, truth be told, Dylan was kind of boring. We'd been going out for so long. It just seemed like the natural next step. More than half of my friends are either engaged or already married."

"Well, it was probably a blessing that you found out sooner rather than later. Now you can move on," Traci said.

"Funny, that's exactly what Jeff said, too. Maybe I should be more like Dan, never get serious about anyone, and just have fun."

There was a knock on the door then and Dan got up to get the pizza while Traci sat thinking about what Suzanne had just said. She'd confirmed what she'd heard about Dan, that he liked to keep things light and wasn't looking to settle down. Maybe she should just back off now before she got in too deep.

Dan returned with the pizza and they all dug in. Traci was quiet as they ate, while Suzanne chattered non-stop and Dan mostly just ate and laughed at the silly stories she was telling, which only encouraged her to keep talking. By the time they finished the pizza and were going to move into the other room to watch a movie, Traci had a splitting headache. She simply wasn't up to staying and spending the evening with Suzanne.

"I'm really beat. It was pretty crazy today. I think I'm going to just head out. You don't mind do you?" she asked Dan, who looked up at her in surprise.

"You're going? Are you sure? You don't want to stay for a movie?"

"No, I'm tired, and you and Suzanne should hang out and catch up. I'm sure I'll see you soon." The words came out a bit stiffly, as both exhaustion and disappointment had taken hold. This was not the evening she'd anticipated.

"Okay, I'll walk you out." Dan turned to Suzanne. "I'll be right back in. Why don't you see what movies are available?"

"Bye, Traci! I hope to see you again." Suzanne called out, and Traci murmured something agreeable as she headed out the door with Dan on her heels.

"Are you okay? I'm so sorry about Suzanne. I had no idea she was coming."

"I'm fine. I really am tired. It's been a long week."

"And this wasn't what you thought tonight would be like."

"That's an understatement." Traci looked into Dan's eyes, wondering how he was feeling about this sudden appearance.

"She's just a friend. There's never been anything between us. She's like a little sister to me."

"Are you sure she feels the same way?"

Dan looked surprised at that and then laughed."She sees me like a brother, too. She and Jeff are just a few years apart and really tight, so we've hung out a lot. She's a good kid." He wrapped his arms around her and pulled her in for a good-night kiss. When they separated, he was smiling. "I've been wanting to do that all night."

Traci relaxed, a little."Okay. I'll see you tomorrow then, for Santa duty?"

"I'll be there at eleven sharp!"

⁂

When Dan came back inside, Suzanne was rummaging through one of his kitchen drawers. She turned when she heard him close the door behind him.

"Hey, do you have a wine opener? Let's open another bottle."

"Sure, hold on. It's over here." The wine opener was still sitting on the island counter top from when they'd opened the bottle that she'd brought earlier in the evening.

"Pick out a bottle. There're a few in the rack. Nothing like what you brought of course, but they're all red."

"After the first bottle, they all taste good anyway," Suzanne said with a laugh as she grabbed one of the bottles.

Dan opened it and over the next few hours as they finished that bottle, Suzanne filled him in on what all his friends had been up to. She said they all missed him terribly, which he found amusing. She also asked about Traci, and if they were serious.

"We haven't been dating long. It's not serious yet, but I really like her."

"She seems nice enough," Suzanne conceded, and then added, "but as long as I've known you, I don't think I've ever seen you get serious with anyone. You always go out with different girls and always seem like you're having fun. I think it's time for me to try that for a while. Just focus on having fun."

Dan thought about that and realized it was true. As long as he'd lived in Chicago, he'd never had a serious relationship. He'd been totally consumed with his work, as were most of his friends, so when they went out at night, they liked to just have a good time. None of the women he'd dated had lasted more than a few months. He'd never really questioned why. It was just always easier to go with the flow, and with the crowd he hung out with, there was no shortage of women to date. Most of the ones he dated were on the same wavelength as him; nothing ever got too deep so there were never any ugly breakup scenes. Though every once in a while, one of the girls he was dating would start to seem like she wanted to get serious or get a bit clingy and that's when he'd just start to distance himself. He just hadn't ever met anyone that he'd wanted to keep seeing for very long. Until now.

The thought of moving back to Chicago was bittersweet. As much as he was looking forward in some ways to going home, he realized that he was going to miss seeing Traci regularly. Lost in his thoughts, he realized Suzanne was still babbling away and he just smiled at her, which was all she seemed to need.

"You're so easy to talk to. Thanks so much for inviting me out here. I really needed to get away." Suzanne was starting to sound tired now and Dan figured the long day of travel and the time difference must have caught up with her. He needed to get to sleep soon, too, or he was going to be one grumpy Santa.

"Are you tired? I think I'm going to head to bed soon."

"Yeah. Suddenly, I'm exhausted."

"Follow me. I'll show you to the guestroom."

Chapter Sixteen

Traci took her time getting ready for Jen's party the next night. She'd called Jen on her way into work that morning, and told her about Dan's unexpected visitor. Jen was fascinated and wanted to hear all about it.

Then she said, "You invited her to the party too, I hope? She has to come. Can't wait to meet them both." Jen always did appreciate the drama in any situation.

"I didn't invite either one of them. I was just thinking I'd come by myself. I was going to invite Dan, but I couldn't do that without inviting her, too, and it was just easier to do nothing."

"Don't be silly. You have to invite them both. She'll love it. There will be tons of people. You know how my parties are."

Yes, she knew and Jen was right, Suzanne would probably love it.

"Fine, I'll see Dan at the store today and will mention it then."

⁂

She didn't have a chance to chat with Dan until mid-afternoon when there was a brief lull and when she mentioned it to him, he thought it sounded like a great idea. He told her he'd been trying to figure out what to do with Suzanne to keep her entertained until she flew home Monday afternoon. Traci gave him Jen's address and let him know she planned on getting there around eight, so they could just meet there. They both had to work until six, so that gave a little time to go home and get ready.

She decided to wear her favorite jeans which were a very dark blue, almost black, and the fabric was extra thin and soft with a little stretch. She loved the way they made her feel and the way they were cut somehow magically made five pounds disappear. Traci picked out a black cashmere sweater that was simple, but flattering. She added her favorite red cowboy boots and was almost ready to go. She was just putting on mascara when there was a light knock on the door, and then it opened and she heard her brother's voice call, "I'm here."

"I'll be down in a sec." She ran a brush through her hair one last time, added a touch of rosy lipstick and then headed down the stairs.

"You look sharp," she greeted Travis, who was wearing a charcoal gray suit with a pale green shirt and tie.

"Thanks. I think I can probably lose the tie though,

right?" Before she could even respond, Travis had pulled the tie loose, unbuttoned two buttons and stuffed the tie in his pocket.

"That feels so much better. Had to come here straight from the office, otherwise I would have changed out of the monkey suit."

"You look great, and you know Jen's parties. There will be a mix of people, some more dressed up than others."

"You look pretty good yourself, are you ready to go?"

✾❦✾

When Travis pulled onto Jen's street, it was immediately clear that the party was well underway. Cars were lined up along both sides of the road leading to her house. They found a spot to park and as they got near the front door, it swung open as someone was stepping outside and Traci could see that Jen's living room was packed. They walked in and Jen came flying over to greet them.

"I'm so glad you're here! Come on in. What are you drinking? Oh, just help yourselves, you know where everything is." Jen darted off again as someone new came through the door.

Traci made her way into the kitchen where Jen had pretty copper tins on the counter filled with ice and assorted beers and there was a row of various red wines, already open, and another tin with ice and a selection of whites. Traci poured herself a glass of Shiraz and Travis helped himself to one of the cold bottles of a local micro-brew.

Aside from Jen, Traci recognized a few familiar faces, but

none that she was dying to go talk to. Instead, she stayed by Travis while he chatted with a couple he knew, a husband and wife who were both attorneys. She guessed that there were at least a hundred or so people here so far, and yet it didn't feel overly crowded. Jen's house had the perfect party layout. It wasn't very big, but the main floor was open concept. It was essentially one really large room with a kitchen in one corner that faced out to the rest of the room.

By 8:30, Dan still hadn't arrived yet, and she wondered if he'd changed his mind, or maybe Suzanne wanted to do something different. But, then, a few minutes later, the door opened and Suzanne made her entrance, followed by Dan.

People stopped and stared when Suzanne walked in looking like she'd stepped out of a fashion magazine. She'd curled her hair, and it fell in tousled waves that fell halfway down her back. But what really got people's attention was her dress, which was candy apple red. It was technically a casual dress. Traci was standing close enough to see that the material was a soft t-shirt like fabric; but the cut was high end. It was sleeveless and dipped low in the front and fell into a draped neckline that was very pretty. When she turned, Traci could see that the back of the dress was where the real drama was. It was almost backless and had the same draped edge that the front did. The dress fell just above her knees and instead of heels, she was also wearing her sleek, black leather cowboy boots. Dan was dressed more casually, in a pair of jeans and a light blue, button down shirt.

Jen hadn't yet met Dan or Suzanne yet, so Traci made her way over to greet them and make the introductions.

"So nice to meet you both. Come on in, help yourselves to drinks in the kitchen," Jen said warmly, then added, "Suzanne, I hear you're just in town for the weekend?"

"That's right, kind of a last minute thing. I needed my Dan fix. I really missed him." She wrapped her arm around his and led him into the next room, where she then poured a glass of wine for herself and asked Dan what kind of beer he wanted.

"This one's good," he said, as he plucked a bottle out of the bin of ice.

Jen shot a look at Traci and raised her eyebrow, to which Traci just shrugged in response. She didn't know what was up with Suzanne's possessive behavior, either. Maybe she was nervous at a party where didn't really know anyone, but somehow Traci doubted that.

"So, how do you like Beauville so far?" Jen asked Suzanne, while keeping one eye on the door for newcomers.

"I haven't seen much of it yet," Suzanne said with a pout. "Dan had to work all day. I still can't believe he, of all people, is playing Santa."

"Just helping out. Traci was in a bind," Dan said as he reached for a cracker and slice of cheese.

"He's doing a great job, and he really saved me," Traci said. "We didn't expect to need a new Santa."

"I have him all to myself on Monday, though." Suzanne lightly touched his arm again. "We're going to do a little sight-seeing, and drive into Bozeman for lunch before I fly out. Oh, and tomorrow night after his shift ends, Dan said he's going to take me to his favorite restaurant here, Delaney's." She looked excited and Traci felt her mood sink a bit. It sounded too much like a date to her.

Dan did at least look somewhat uncomfortable at the attention. "It's Delancey's, and Traci, we hope you can come to dinner, too, if you're not busy?"

As much as she hated the thought of the two of them going out to dinner together, Traci really had no desire to join them, not if Suzanne was going to be there to monopolize the conversation.

"That sounds great, but I have plans to have dinner with my parents tomorrow." That wasn't quite true yet, but Traci knew if she dropped by in the afternoon, that her mother would insist that she stay for dinner.

"So, I'll have you all to myself. That will be fun, then." Suzanne shot Traci a sweet smile. "I'll take good care of him for you."

"I think I need more wine." Traci went to top off her glass and take a break from Suzanne if only for a moment. Travis was leaning on the counter, watching the crowd with a look of amusement. The couple he'd been chatting with had wandered off and Travis looked like he was taking it all in. His demeanor suddenly changed as Traci walked over towards him. He stood up straight suddenly and ran a hand through his hair. She thought that seemed odd, but then a moment later, Traci heard a familiar voice behind her, and understood why.

"Hi, Traci, Travis, nice to see you both here." Traci turned to see Isabella standing there wearing a Winter white sweater dress that hugged her curves, with soft, camel colored dress boots. Her hair was about the same length as Suzanne's, but was so dark brown that it was almost black and fell in natural loose curls about her shoulders. Her lipstick was a rich burgundy red, which made her perfect teeth appear even whiter. As usual, around Isabella, Traci felt a bit mousy in comparison.

Isabella chatted with Dan about a few real estate deals that she had in the process of closing; as her attorney, he handled all the legal paperwork that was required. Traci was half-listening as her eyes followed Suzanne and Dan around the room. You'd never know that the two of them barely knew anyone here by the way they were chatting up a storm with people they'd just met, and mingling so easily. Suddenly, though, Isabella drew her attention after she stopped her conversation with Travis mid-sentence to exclaim, "Who is that?"

Traci looked toward the front door where Isabella was openly staring in admiration. A very tall, easily 6' 4" or so, rugged, yet stunningly beautiful man stood just inside the doorway and was glancing around the room, looking for someone. His very blonde hair looked like it could use a trim, and there was a hint of stubble on his chin, but the look worked for him, especially combined with a square jaw and piercing pale blue eyes. He was wearing jeans, a plain black t-shirt, and a well-worn brown leather jacket. Jen was nearby and turned toward the door to see what the fuss was about and Traci noticed with interest that her friend looked completely shocked and for a long moment was speechless, something Traci hadn't seen in years.

"Ian," she said softly.

His eyes met hers and a wide grin stretched across his face, sending a spray of laugh lines dancing around his eyes and mouth.

He walked toward her, leaned over, picked her up and kissed her hard; then set her down again.

"You told me you were having a party," he said, with a twinkle in his eye.

"I never...I mean...I only emailed you yesterday afternoon. How did you manage to make it here so quickly?"

"They do have planes in Ireland, you know." He grinned again and pulled her in for another hug. "We got our release done earlier than expected, so I was able to arrange for a few days off."

"Well, come in. I'll introduce you to everyone. I can't believe you're really here."

She led him over to Traci, Travis and Isabella and said, "This is Ian McKendrick. We met in Ireland. He was very helpful with some of my research." Traci noticed that a slight blush had crept onto Jen's cheeks. It wasn't like her to be this flustered, and Traci found it fascinating.

"Ian, this is Traci, my best friend, her brother Travis, and my sister, Isabella." By that time, Suzanne and Dan had made their way around the room, so Jen introduced them, too. "And this is Traci's friend Dan, and his friend Suzanne who is also in town for a few days."

Suzanne was the first to speak. "It's so nice to meet you. I love your accent!" She nudged Isabella out of her way and reached out to stroke Ian's jacket. "I love this, too. Is it a Bendy? He does amazing work."

Ian looked at her in confusion. "I have no idea. What is a Bendy?"

"Oh, never mind."

"If you'd all excuse us, I'm going to introduce Ian to everyone." Jen led Ian into the crowd. Traci couldn't wait to catch up with her tomorrow and get the full scoop on Ian McKendrick.

Isabella looked like she had something on her mind, and Traci wasn't surprised when she asked Dan, "Where's Christian tonight?"

"He's out of town this weekend," Dan said. He didn't elaborate, which Traci thought was nice of him. Why mention that he went to Manhattan? Her brother, however, had no issue sharing the information.

"He's in Manhattan. I heard from him about an hour ago. He's staying out there until Thursday and then he and Molly are flying back together on Friday." Travis said.

"Molly's coming back?" Isabella looked genuinely surprised.

"They worked things out. With her job, too. Her old boss is going to fill in for her and train her replacement. Turns out the hotel he was going to move to has construction delays or something like that. Anyway, she doesn't have to stick around there; he told her she could head back in time for Christmas."

"That's wonderful!" Traci was thrilled for both of them.

"Yeah, that's really great." Isabella agreed, then said, "If you'll excuse me, I see someone I need to talk to."

"Is she still hung up on Christian, do you think?" Traci asked her brother quietly.

He was thoughtful for a moment, then said, "I don't know. I kind of doubt it. I don't think they ever really were that crazy about each other. Isabella just doesn't like to lose. She likes to be in control of when things end."

"You still have a crush on her," Traci announced, but not loudly enough that anyone else could hear her. "So, when are you going to do something about it?"

"Just biding my time, waiting for the right moment."

"Are you sure about this? Isabella, of all people?" Traci somehow just couldn't see her brother with her, either. They seemed to be such opposites. Where Isabella was so outgoing and dramatic, her brother was reserved, intense even, and definitely conservative.

"You just don't know her the way I do. She's a great girl."

"Okay, I'll take your word for that. She's Jen's sister, after all."

Dan walked over to her then and looked as though he wanted to talk. Travis picked up on it, too, and murmured something about wanting to mingle. Suzanne was nowhere to be seen.

"Did you lose Suzanne?" she teased.

"She said something about needing to use the bathroom. I think we have a few minutes to ourselves."

"How's it going having a houseguest?"

Dan's expression was a mix of irritation and embarrassment. "I'm not used to it. Not used to having anyone around like that. Especially someone like Suzanne. I love her, but she's a handful."

"High maintenance?" Traci tried not to laugh.

"Yeah, a bit. She's a good kid, though. I think she was

more upset about the breakup than she let on. It's nice to see her, but I am looking forward to having my house back."

"Here she comes, time to change the subject." Suzanne was heading their way, with newly fluffed hair and a fresh coat of lipstick.

"When can I see you this week?"

Before Traci could answer, Suzanne was beside them.

"Everyone is so friendly here!" she said as she added more wine to her empty glass.

"People are really friendly here," Dan agreed. "It's been so long since I've spent much time here, that I'd forgotten that."

"It just seems so quiet here, though. I bet you're dying to get home." Then she glanced at Traci and added, "No offense meant."

"None taken."

"It's just that there's been so much going on back home. Tons of holiday parties." She grew silent for a moment, then added, "I almost forgot, though, you don't usually go to any of those."

"No, not usually. It's been nice being home, actually, catching up with family. And making new friends." He pulled Traci in close to him and Suzanne looked bored again.

"I'm going to wander. Back in a bit."

"So, you never did tell me, when can I see you this week? Monday night?"

"Monday's already out, how's Tuesday?"

"Perfect. I have an idea. Do you like to go bowling?"

Traci laughed. "I haven't done that in years."

"Let's go bowling, it'll be fun. I don't suppose there's anywhere to bowl here in Beauville?"

"No, we have to go to Bozeman for that."

"It'll be fun. We'll find somewhere interesting to grab a bite after."

"I'm not even sure if I remember how to bowl!" Traci loved the idea, though. It sounded like something fun and different.

"No worries. I'll give you a private lesson."

Chapter Seventeen

We're going bowling!" Traci couldn't help smiling as she said it. She was having breakfast at the Morning Muffin with Jen before her Tuesday morning shift at the store. Jen had called just as she was getting out of bed and said she was dying to talk to her. But, so far, Traci had done most of the talking.

"That sounds like so much fun. I haven't done that in a million years," Jen said as she broke off a piece of her triple-berry scone and popped it in her mouth.

"Neither have I. Sounds like Dan has, though. He said he'll give me a private lesson."

Jen raised her eyebrow at that and Traci laughed. "So, enough about me, spill. I haven't talked to you since the party. Tell me everything."

"Okay. Well, he just left at the crack of dawn this morning. Earlier actually; it was still dark out."

"He really lives in Ireland? And flew over for your party? Who is this guy?"

"Ian McKendrick lives just outside Dublin and owns one of the hottest software companies in Ireland. Something to do with clouds and the internet."

"Cloud computing. I don't know a thing about it, but I have heard that it's one of the hot technologies."

"He founded it with his partner five years ago, and it took off a year later. He's a smart guy."

"Must be to do that. How did you meet him?"

Jen laughed. " At a bar. I know, it's the oldest cliché in the world. He literally bumped into me at this little neighborhood pub near the house I was renting. He was walking in as I was walking toward my seat at the bar. His phone was ringing and he wasn't paying attention and slammed right into me. I'd just ordered a new beer and he knocked the glass right out of my hand. Made quite a mess."

"So he bought you a new one?"

"He bought me drinks the rest of the night. He felt so bad about it. As it turned out, we had a few things in common."

"Yeah, like what?"

Jen thought for a minute and then laughed again. "Okay, we have nothing in common, but we had a blast together and there seems to be an attraction."

"Seems to be? That guy is hot, and he looked like he was very interested in you, too."

"He does seem to be. It's been a bit of a whirlwind. We met two weeks before I was due to fly back and I saw him almost every day before I left. I have plans to head back there in about six weeks for more research, but he said he couldn't possibly wait that long. I mentioned the party in an email to him and told him he was invited, but it was kind of a joke...I never thought he'd actually come." She was quiet then for a moment, chewing on her scone, lost in her thoughts. Then she added, "I'm really glad that he did, though. He was able to stay through the weekend and I showed him all around."

"Did you introduce him to your parents?"

"I did. He had booked a room at Isabella's bed and breakfast, so I was able to tell them that, to ease their minds. It would have freaked them out even more if I'd said I'd invited a hot Irish guy that I'd just met over here, and spent the weekend in bed with him.

"It's that serious already?" Traci wasn't really that surprised.

"We slept together the first night we met." That did surprise her. At the shocked look on Traci's face, Jen laughed and explained. "He was my first one-night stand and it didn't go quite as planned. I just decided to go for it, thinking I'd just had the most fun night ever with the hottest guy I'd ever met and since I was sort of on vacation, I figured why not live a little?"

"So, he didn't get the memo about it being a one night stand?" Traci teased.

"No. He asked for my number when he left in the morning and called later that afternoon to take me out to dinner. I'd told him I was only there for two more weeks and he said he didn't want to waste a day. It was the best two weeks of my life."

"Now I know why you're going back for more research."

"Well, I really do want to go visit some of the castles I didn't get to see. I have a new idea I'm toying with. Plus, who am I kidding? I can't wait to go back there and play some more."

"Is this serious, then?"

Jen thought about that for a minute. "I don't know what it is. We live in different countries. This might just be a really fun fling for both of us. I want to take it day by day and just enjoy his company while I'm there."

"I'm really happy for you. I've never seen you like this before."

"Well, what about you and Dan? How's that going?"

"I'm not sure. I was really enjoying his company, too, as long as I don't think about the fact that he's just here temporarily. Plus, Suzanne dropping in like this just reminded me of what I've heard about Dan. He moves in a different crowd than I do. He's used to hanging out with girls like Suzanne, who have trust funds, and I heard he's dated his share of models. Dan's a catch and he's never been interested in settling down. I just don't want to get too attached."

"Dan doesn't strike me as a snob. He just happens to have a job that pays well. Doesn't mean it defines who he is. And maybe he's never shown an interest in settling down because he just hasn't found the right one yet. It could be you."

"I don't know about that."

"Well, you should find out. Go bowling, have fun. Live it up a little. Have crazy monkey sex." At Traci's shocked expression Jen laughed out loud. "I highly recommend it."

Traci glanced at the clock and realized she'd have to run

to get to work on time. "I have to go! I'll catch up with you later." She stood up and gathered her empty coffee cup and paper plate to toss in the trash.

Jen pulled a laptop out of her bag and set it on the table. She looked up at Traci, "I'm going to sit here a bit and do some writing. Remember what I said, just do it already. See if the attraction is there."

✳✳✳

Crazy monkey sex. Every time Traci thought of what Jen had said earlier, it made her smile. She and Dan had just arrived at the bowling alley in Bozeman and she was looking forward to their evening.

"What's so funny?" Dan asked.

"Oh nothing, just thinking of something Jen said earlier. She cracks me up. I'm so glad that she's back."

"What size shoe do you need?" The cashier asked.

"Oh, an eight, please." Traci removed her shoes while Dan paid the cashier for their shoe rentals and two games. They headed to one of the lanes and each picked out a ball.

She watched as Dan demonstrated the proper way to hold and then throw the ball. His ball slid perfectly down the middle of the line and knocked down nine pins. Almost a strike.

"Okay, your turn," he said. She grabbed hold of her ball and attempted to throw it just the way she'd seen Dan do it. But her ball wobbled down the center lane then veered off to the left and into the gutter.

"Oops."

"No worries, you're just rusty. Try it again."

Her next attempts were better, and after the first few strings she started to settle in and enjoy herself. After they finished their second game, they turned in their shoes and headed out to Mac Brothers pub for burgers. Traci had been dying for a good burger and knew Dan would like this place. "So, I think I'm going to be heading back to Chicago soon," Dan said while they waited for their food to arrive. This was the moment she had been dreading.

"Have you decided on a date?"

"Well, New Year's Eve falls on a Saturday night this year, so I was thinking of heading back the night before or morning of, not sure on that yet. It will depend on what's available for flights."

"That's less than two weeks away."

"I know. I was planning on going around the beginning of the year, and when Suzanne mentioned her New Year's Eve party, I thought it might be fun to be back for that."

"For Suzanne's party." Secretly she'd hoped that Dan might still be in Beauville then.

"For New Year's Eve. It's a blast in Chicago."

"I'm sure it is. It sounds like an exciting city." Disappointment was starting to seep in. Her time with Dan was running out. She stared into her beer, and then took another sip. Dan reached out and grabbed hold of one of her hands.

"I was kind of hoping you might want to come with me. Fly back and spend the weekend. We can ring in the New Year together." He sounded excited, but when Traci was silent, he added, "If you're interested. I really think we'd have a blast."

"Okay." She tried not to let her disappointment about him leaving show.

"Okay, you'll come?"

She smiled up at him. "Yes, I'd love to. I've never been to Chicago."

"Great, I'll get our tickets in the morning. I can't wait to show you the city."

Their burgers came, then and they dug in. Traci really was excited to go to Chicago with Dan, to see where he lived and what his life was like there. She was going to try to relax, take Jen's advice and just enjoy their time together.

They went back to his house after dinner. Traci settled comfortably on his sofa while Dan ran to the kitchen to get something. He came back a minute later with two glasses of milk and a plate of homemade chocolate chip cookies.

"Mrs. O'Brien dropped these off earlier today. I think she's trying to fatten me up."

Traci reached for one and took a bite. "So good!" Dan reached for one, too, and then settled in close to Traci on the sofa and put his arm around her. He clicked on the TV until he found a soft music channel, then focused his attention on Traci.

"Suzanne really put a damper on my plans for us this weekend. I wanted to spend more time with you."

"I did, too."

"I've been thinking a lot about this all weekend, and I don't want to just have you come visit me and then that's it. I haven't been serious with anyone in a long time, but if you're up for it, I want to try, to see if we can make the long-distance thing work. I can come back here for some weekends or you could come to Chicago. I just know I'm not ready to stop spending time with you."

Traci's heart jumped. It sounded like she and Dan were on the same wave-length after all. Maybe they could make some kind of a long-distance relationship work.

"And I know I've been dying to do this for days now." He leaned over and kissed her, and Traci felt a thrill run through her. Yes, there was a very strong attraction here. She ran her fingers softly through his hair as he pulled her more tightly to him. She drew her breath in when he gently pushed her hair off to the side and then moved his lips to her neck and then kissed his way along her jaw until he was back on her mouth again. He deepened the kiss and they continued kissing like that for a while, until Dan pulled back and said, "Do you want to get more comfortable?" He was smiling and his sexy, yet boyishly hopeful expression did it for her. She was ready for more. She nodded and he stood and held out his hand and then led her into his bedroom.

They slept in the next morning. When Traci woke, Dan's leg was tangled with hers. She reached for his cellphone on the nightstand next to her, to check the time. It was still early, but she needed to go soon to get ready for work. She shifted a little and then Dan rolled on to his side. "Morning," he said sleepily. "What time is it? Do we need to go soon?"

"It's a little before seven, and unfortunately, yes, I have to be in by nine."

Dan snapped awake and swung his legs off the side of the bed.

"Okay, give me five minutes to get dressed and we can head out." He pulled his pants on and then disappeared into the bathroom. Traci slid out of bed and dressed quickly as well, and was ready to go when Dan came back in the room.

Ten minutes later they pulled into Traci's driveway. Dan reached over and pulled her in for a hug and a sweet, short kiss.

"I'll call you later this afternoon."

The rest of the week flew by. Traci spent every night with Dan. While she wouldn't quite describe their love-making as 'crazy monkey sex', it was wonderful and she looked forward to every minute she had with him. He seemed to feel the same way. At the end of each day, they checked in with each other and either he came to her place for the evening or she went to his. She did notice, though, that as Christmas crept up, he seemed to be a bit quieter, more distant. She'd assumed that he would come to the Christmas Eve service that Saturday and then they'd go on to Christian's open house after that. He and Molly were due back sometime Friday evening and Dan had mentioned that Mrs. O'Brien had been bustling around all week cooking up a storm, and making arrangements for the gathering. She and Dan were at his place Friday night and had just finished a pizza and were about to settle on the sofa and watch a movie when Traci brought up their Christmas Eve plans.

"So, the store closes at three tomorrow. The service with the children's pageant is at five and then we can just head over to the open house after that. I have to be there a little earlier to help the kids get ready, so you might want to go with Molly and Christian and I'll meet you afterward."

Dan was quiet for a moment, and just sat there clicking the remote over and over again and watching different channels go by.

"I think I'll probably skip the church service tomorrow. I'm not sure about the open house."

"What? Are you serious?"

"I don't typically do Christmas," he reminded her. He had a sullen expression that Traci hadn't seen before.

She sat next to him on the sofa and put her hand on his knee.

"You've been living in a Santa suit for the past few weekends. How can you say you don't 'do Christmas'," she teased.

That got a small smile out of him. "That was just for you, to help you."

"I think it's helped you a little too, though. You have to admit, you've kind of enjoyed playing Santa."

"That's true, but it's different. I'm starting to get that same feeling I get every year when Christmas is almost here, like I just want to stay inside now until it's over. It's hard to explain."

"Maybe you just need to face it head on, to start participating in the holidays more. Try to find the joy in the day, and refuse to accept the pain anymore."

"You just don't understand. It's not that easy."

"Sometimes the things we need to do aren't easy. But the

first time will be the hardest. It will get easier after that. I think."

"Right, you think. You haven't been here, you don't know. What if it makes everything worse?"

"Well, I suppose it might. But how will you know if you don't at least try?"

"I don't know. I can't tell you right now that I'll go, because I don't know that I will." He continued to click the remote and Traci was starting to get annoyed. She understood that this time of year was hard for him, but she thought he was being a bit of a baby about it to not even want to try.

"Well, maybe I should leave you alone so you can think this through." Traci stood up and walked towards her bag and pulled on her jacket.

"You're leaving?" Dan sounded angry now and Traci realized they were having their first fight. She really thought he was being unreasonable, though.

"This is important to me, and I think it's something you need to try to get past."

"Maybe you should go, then. I'm not going to be forced into doing anything."

"I'm not trying to force you. I'm just telling you how I feel and that's obviously not important enough to you. I'll see you at the store tomorrow."

"Fine." He looked miserable, and Traci was tempted to stay but sensed that it wouldn't help matters, so she zipped up her coat and braced herself to face the cold.

Chapter Eighteen

The store was insanely busy the next day, packed with last-minute shoppers. Traci didn't stop all day, except for a quick fifteen minute break for lunch where she inhaled a sandwich in the back room and then jumped right back on the floor. She could have taken a longer break, but it just didn't feel right with the store being so busy.

From what she could see, Dan didn't even stop for a lunch break. The line was never-ending and she didn't have a chance to talk to him at all until the store had closed and they were both walking out the door.

"So, what did you decide?" she asked as they reached their cars.

He still looked miserable and exhausted from the day.

"I thought about it all last night, and I'm sorry, but I just don't think I can do it. It's not you at all. It's just…I don't know. I guess I'm just not up for it."

Traci said nothing. She'd hoped and really thought that he'd come around, especially knowing how important the holidays were to her.

"I did get you a Christmas gift, though. I know you're probably with your family on Christmas, so if you want to come by Monday night, that could work."

"I got you a gift, too, but I don't really care about that. The best gift you could have given me was just to be there, with me."

"I'm really sorry."

"I guess I'll see you Monday, then," she said as she unlocked her car and then looked back at him. "Merry Christmas, Dan."

He just smiled back at her, with a sad look in his eyes.

Dan felt like shit as he watched Traci leave. He drove home and jumped in the shower, hoping the hot water would wash away his bad mood. It didn't. He dressed and then wandered into the kitchen, thought about having a beer, then decided against it, knowing it would likely only make his dark mood worse. He didn't feel like being alone, though, as his thoughts weren't good company at the moment. He was waging an internal war with himself, debating whether or not to take Traci's advice and try to face the holiday head on for the first time in years.

He decided to head next door and see what Christian and

Molly were up to. Mrs. O'Brien was just heading out as he walked in, off to spend the holiday with her family.

"Merry Christmas, Dan!" she said when she saw him.

"Same to you."

"You off to church with Molly and Christian soon? Everything is all set for the open house now. It should be their biggest, merriest one yet."

"I'm not sure, haven't decided yet," he admitted.

Mrs. O'Brien's face clouded. "I don't want to tell you what to do, but I think you should go. It would mean a lot to everyone, but especially to yourself. Could be there's a reason why you're here now. I think your parents are up there, watching over you, and I truly believe they'd want you to go. Well, that's my two cents anyway. You do what you want." She gave him a hug then and was on her way. Dan sighed and walked through the door.

Molly and Christian were both in the kitchen. Christian was fiddling with a necktie while Molly bustled around, organizing and arranging things for the gathering later. When she saw Dan standing in the doorway, she ran over and gave him a hug.

"Merry Christmas! You're coming with us, right? We're going to head out to the church in about twenty minutes."

"It's a good idea to get there early if we want to get decent seats," Christian explained.

Dan ignored the question, and instead said, "Molly, it's great to see you back here. I'm so glad you guys worked things out."

Molly beamed and then said, "Christian proposed in Manhattan and we're getting married for real."

"That's great!"

"It's just going to be a very small service, immediate family and a few close friends," Christian said. "I'd love to have you stand up for me this time."

"I'd be honored to." Dan had missed their first wedding as he'd been out of the country on assignment in London for one of the financial magazines that he still wrote for occasionally. He'd wanted to fly back, but Christian had talked him out of it and explained that it wasn't a 'real' wedding, so there wasn't anything to rush back for.

The mood and look of the house was bright and cheery and festive. A huge, real tree sat in the corner of the family room and was beautifully decorated and twinkling with colored lights. A sprig of mistletoe hung above the doorway, which Christian said was the idea spot as it was such a high traffic area and would be a lot of fun once the party got underway. Both Molly and Christian radiated joy and contentment and Dan thought about going back to his place, which was empty and cold in comparison, except for the little tree that Traci had brought him. If he didn't go with them, and stayed home, that tree would be a constant reminder of Traci and of what he was giving up by not going. Something shifted inside him, and a decision was made.

"So, who's driving?"

Christian drove, and when they walked into the church, Dan was surprised to see that it was already three quarters full. Christian led them down toward the front and found a pew that had room for the three of them. Dan looked around for Traci but there was no sign of her.

The church was full within ten minutes and by a few minutes to five, it was already at standing room only capacity. At five o'clock on the dot, the music began and Dan saw Traci step towards the front of the church. She was slightly off to the side so she wouldn't be in the way, but close enough to help the children if they got stuck and keep things moving along.

Within minutes, Dan found himself caught up in the story. He'd only seen the tail end of the pageant when he stopped by the rehearsal a few weeks back. He glanced around the church at one point and was moved by the expressions on everyone's face. They were all caught up in the story as well and once again, when the music started for *Silent Night* and the children began singing, Dan felt that same surge of joy and blissful peace wash over him and through him. It was stronger than before and the feeling of calm was more clear. He couldn't explain what it was but it felt almost as if something had lifted and he had a strong sense of someone saying, "It's okay." He didn't understand it, but yet on some level, he did. Whether it was a message from God or his own subconscious, the meaning was clear. It was time to let go of the past, to move on and embrace the future. To be joyous. He also felt relief. A big part of the reason he'd been reluctant to come had been fear. He didn't know how he was going to react, and now that he knew, it was as if a big weight had been lifted.

At the end of the service, they followed the crowd outside and while they were chatting with fellow parishioners and wishing each other a Merry Christmas, Dan kept scanning the crowd for a glimpse of Traci. Finally, she came through the door, with her coat wrapped tightly around her. She didn't see him until she was almost directly in front of him and when she finally did, she stopped in her tracks.

"You're here." Her voice was soft and uncertain, a bit hesitant.

Dan pulled her aside so they could talk privately.

"You were right, I needed to come. And I'm so glad I did. Thank you."

"So, you're feeling okay? It wasn't too difficult?"

"No, it was wonderful actually. You were amazing, the kids were great. I'm really glad I came. I think it helped."

Traci looked relieved and very happy to hear that.

"And the open house? Are you going to that, too?"

"I wouldn't miss it. I'll see you there."

Chapter Nineteen

Traci was beyond thrilled that Dan had decided to come to church and to attend the open house. She had been feeling really down about their fight the night before and wasn't looking forward to not seeing him on Christmas. Her original plan was to go right to the open house from church, but now that Dan was going to be there, she decided to stop home first and pick up his gift.

When she finally arrived at Christian and Molly's house, the party was well under way and the kitchen was full of people talking and mixing drinks. Dan saw her when she walked in and came rushing over to greet her.

"Go back out and come back in again."

"What?"

"Just do it." He was grinning at her, so she obliged by taking a few steps back and then walked through the door again.

"Okay, stop right there?"

"What are you doing?" She was confused, and curious.

"Look up." She did and smiled when she saw the large sprig of mistletoe dangling above them.

"Not that it's necessary, but it's kind of fun." He pulled her in then and kissed her, and his kiss was both tender and urgent. Neither one of them wanted to stop, but since they had an audience, they kept it short.

"I missed you," Dan said.

"I haven't gone anywhere." Tracie gave him another quick kiss.

"It was the thought of not seeing you that made me realize I'd just miss you too much. Christmas has been hard enough in recent years. I think it would be even harder if you weren't with me."

"I'm so happy that you changed your mind. I would have really missed you, too."

"Stay with me tonight. I want to give you your gift later, when we're alone."

"I have yours with me, too."

They spent the next few hours having a great time, with family and friends. Her brother, Travis, and her parents came by for a while as did Molly's mother and Aunt Betty. They were both so excited to have Molly back in Beauville, close to them, and back together with Christian.

"I knew they'd end up together," Aunt Betty said at one point when she was chatting with Traci and Jen.

"I thought you were all excited about the architect she was going on a date with?" Traci teased.

"No, she belongs with Christian. Look how happy they both are."

Traci agreed with her there. She'd never seen the two of them so relaxed and happy. Her friend, Jen, on the other hand, wasn't her usual cheery self.

"Is everything okay?" Traci asked her when Aunt Betty had wandered off and they were alone for a moment.

"Oh, it's fine. I'm just missing Ian and a little blue that he's not here. But of course he's with his family in Ireland, and I'll be with mine tomorrow, so it's all good." Traci gave her a hug. "Well, I'm so glad that you're here."

"Thanks. Maybe I need another glass of champagne, with a strawberry in it this time. That should cheer me up!" The champagne was flowing and seemed to be the drink of choice, either right out of the bottle or in the giant bowl of champagne punch that had rainbow sherbet floating on top. Traci decided to try a glass of it.

A few hours later, as the party was starting to wind down, Dan found her and suggested they head back to his place. Once there, he went into his office and came back with a giant box that was about two feet square and looked heavy. It was beautifully wrapped and had a shiny gold bow on top.

"Go ahead, open it." His eyes danced as she picked up the package, wondering what it could possibly be. She undid the wrapping and opened the box. Something large and square was wrapped in tissue paper. She pulled it out and her eyes teared up at his thoughtfulness. She was holding a binder filled with large squares of color samples, thick paper that had actually been painted with different colors. There were over a hundred of them.

"Now you can bring that to your decorating jobs and

help clients see what the colors will really look like once their walls are painted."

"Thank you so much. This is such a great idea. How did you ever think of it?"

"I remembered when you and I were first talking about colors for the different rooms that I'd gone online and stumbled across this. I didn't think anything of it at the time, but remembered it when I was trying to think of what to get you."

"I love it."

"That's not all, though. There's something else in there. Did you see the small box?" Traci hadn't noticed anything else in the box. She looked again and moved aside a piece of tissue and there was a very small box, a jewelry box. She pulled it out and opened it. Inside was a diamond tennis bracelet. It was stunning, and it was definitely too much.

"This is beautiful, but it's too extravagant. I can't accept this. You shouldn't be spending this kind of money on me."

"I want to, and can easily afford to do so. You're important to me. I wanted to get you something special."

"Well, I love it of course, but what I got you just seems so small now."

"Don't be ridiculous. Whatever you got me is bound to be perfect."

"It's not even in the same league, but I hope you like it." Traci handed him his gift and waited as he unwrapped it. The first thing he lifted out of the box was a feather soft cashmere sweater. It was dark green and had a v-neck that she knew would look great on him. She hoped that he'd think of her when he wore it.

"This is great. I don't have many sweaters like this. I like that it's nice and thin, almost more like a shirt. I'll think of you when I wear it." He leaned over and kissed her.

"There's something else in there, too, something small that I made for you."

"You made me something?" He reached back in the box and pulled out a photo album with a brown, buttery soft leather cover. Dan flipped it open and looked through the pages. Traci had filled it with pictures of them and all of their friends and the places they'd visited during his stay here. He finally closed it and then drew Traci in close for a hug and kiss.

"This is the best thing you could have given me. It's perfect, and I love that you made it." He paused then and added, "I love you. I just want you to know that. The time we've spent together these past few months have been really special. I don't want it to stop."

"I don't either. I love you, too." It sounded funny to say the words, but Traci recognized that she'd felt this way for weeks now and had been fighting it. A long distance relationship wasn't ideal, but plenty of people did it, so it could be done.

"Now, let's go to bed and celebrate properly. I believe it's officially Christmas now." The clock on the TV confirmed that it was indeed a few minutes past twelve.

"Merry Christmas!" Traci said as she reached for his hand and they walked toward the bedroom.

❄❅❄

The week between Christmas and New Year's Eve was bittersweet for Traci. She loved spending as much time as possible with Dan and was looking forward to traveling with him to Chicago for the weekend, but she was not looking forward to the weeks after that, when they'd be so far apart. She just kept reminding herself that other people made it work, so they could, too.

When they left late afternoon on Friday the weather was clear and sunny, and although there were no non-stop flights available they didn't have a long layover at all and both flights were smooth. An hour later, after getting their bags from the luggage area and finding a cab, they arrived at Dan's condo a little after eight.

When Dan had told her that he had a condo in an old brownstone building in Chicago, Traci had envisioned a small, sparsely decorated place, nothing fancy. She had friends who lived in New York City, including Molly, who had often talked about how tiny the apartments were and she assumed that it would be similar in Chicago. But Dan's place was not small. It was on the fourth floor, and the building was so old that there was no elevator, so she was glad that she had only brought a small carryon bag with her. Dan had one large suitcase that he slowly carried up. Once they were on the fourth floor, she was surprised to see that there were only two apartments. All the other floors had at least six, she'd noticed, as they made their way up.

Dan opened the door and let Traci walk in first. She took a few steps in and then set down her bag and looked around. This was nothing like what she'd expected. She realized that Dan's little stock business must be doing very well. She'd never really thought about it before. She just knew that Dan worked alone and spent most of his time glued to the computer, watching stocks and then writing about his thoughts after the day was done.

The room she was standing in was truly spectacular. Dan explained that the two apartments on the fourth floor were the penthouse units. He showed her around, and the decorator in her marveled at the gorgeous design and striking colors that he had chosen. He admitted that he'd had a decorator do it all for him. The walls were a mix of cool gray and pale copper. The hardwood floors gleamed and tall, floor to ceiling windows let in plenty of light. The ceilings were high and though it wasn't a loft, it had that kind of a feel to it with a roomy, open layout and a kitchen that faced the entertainment/family room. Traci knew Dan enjoyed cooking when he had the time, and the kitchen reflected that. The countertops were black granite and the backsplash was white Calcutta marble subway tiles. Stainless steel appliances and pale gray cabinets completed the cool, crisp look.

There was a working fireplace in the center of the room that was double-sided and an area off to the side where he had wood neatly stacked. There were two bedrooms and Dan led her into the master bedroom which was enormous and had walls that were painted a deep charcoal gray with blue tones. The rest of the room followed suit in varying shades of blue and gray. The overall feel was restful and almost cave-like, as he also had opaque shades that were drawn to keep out the light.

He then led her back into the main area and around a corner where he had his office set up. Four full-size monitors sat on a sleek, black glass desk with a printer and file cabinet to the right. When she saw all the four monitors, she laughed and said, "How did you ever get by with just two monitors in Beauville?"

He just smiled and said, "I had to adapt."

They walked through French doors next that led out to a private terrace, which overlooked the city and had rows of pots lined up on each side. Dan explained that in the warmer weather he kept plants out there and had experimented with growing fresh tomatoes and herbs.

"I wasn't always good about remembering to water them. Let's just say I don't have a green thumb yet."

As they walked back into the condo, Dan's phone started buzzing. He answered it and it sounded like one of his friends looking to make plans. He covered the phone for a moment and asked, "That's my buddy Jeff on the line, wanting to know if we want to meet up downtown for a few drinks. There's a new place that just opened that he says makes a great martini. I'm sure they have good wine, too."

"Sure, that sounds fun." Traci would have rather stayed in with Dan, but knew her time here in Chicago was limited and it might be good to meet his friends tonight so she wouldn't be meeting them for the first time at Suzanne's party.

They both felt grimy from flying and took turns showering quickly. The hot water felt wonderful and Traci enjoyed the great water pressure and was fascinated by the body sprays in the shower that sent out a warm mist everywhere. The bathroom was gorgeous, too, with an all glass shower and smooth marble floors. She changed while Dan showered and since she wasn't sure how dressy the place was that they were going to and Dan had never been there, she decided on black dress pants, and low slung heels that were flattering but low enough that she could still walk easily. She added a thin, shimmery silver sweater that was festive and sparkly and then went off to blow dry her hair and do her makeup.

Twenty minutes later, they were both ready. Dan had called ahead and there was a car waiting for them downstairs. Dan was also wearing dress pants and a bright red shirt. The two of them together looked very holiday appropriate, Traci thought to herself as they climbed into the car.

Fifteen minutes later, the driver pulled in front of a busy restaurant and confirmed that it was the right place.

Dan led her inside and, once in, he looked around to see if Jeff was already there. The restaurant was packed and the hostess at the reception desk indicated that there was a large bar area on the second floor and pointed them toward a metal spiral staircase. They made their way through the crowd and up the stairs. It was somewhat less crowded as there was no eating on this floor, just a long winding stainless steel bar and tall cocktail tables scattered throughout the room.

"Over here!" A voice called out from the far corner. A dark-haired guy about Dan's age was waving at them. Dan's face lit up when he saw him and they headed over.

"So glad you both could make it! It's been way too long." The person that Traci assumed was Jeff drew Dan in for a hug and pat on the back.

"Traci, this is Jeff, and you already know Suzanne." There were several others that he also introduced her, too, and she recognized some of the names from stories he'd told her about his friends. Jeff and Toby ran a hedge fund together and Suzanne and her best friend April, who was also Toby's girlfriend, were both involved with the same charity that the New Year's Eve party was going to benefit.

"Great to see you again, Traci. Pull up a chair and join us," Suzanne said. Dan pulled chairs over for both of them and then ordered a round of drinks for everyone when the cocktail waitress came by. Since everyone was drinking martinis here, Traci decided to follow suit and ordered a cosmopolitan. She didn't generally drink vodka as it tended to hit her harder than a glass of wine ever would, but she figured one would be okay and she could enjoy it and then switch to wine if she wanted a second drink. She took a small sip when the drink arrived and was surprised by how delicious it was. It had been a long time she'd had one and must have forgotten how good they could be.

"They make the best cosmos here," Suzanne said as Traci took another sip of her drink. "The bartender told me that they make their own simple syrup and infuse it with orange oil."

Traci sat next to Dan for the next few hours, mostly listening to the conversation swirling around her, enjoying her cocktail and taking it all in. These people had known each other for years, and although they included her in the conversation, she didn't feel like she had much to contribute and mostly just nodded and asked a question here and there. Truth be told, she was a bit intimidated by some of the comments that raced by.

"So, we sold our stake in that company I'd told you about and cleared a cool twenty mil," Jeff said at one point. Toby immediately jumped in and added, "Yeah, and Dan, that company you told us to keep an eye on, the one that had a killer pattern forming? We got in at just the right time and sold out three weeks later and more than doubled our money. That one was huge."

"Traci, have you been to Monte Carlo?" Suzanne asked.

"No, no I haven't." Traci had never been out of the country, let alone to Monte Carlo.

"You should totally go. We went a few months ago and it's phenomenal."

"Well, it helps not having a job," April said. "Otherwise, we couldn't just take off like that."

"Wait until you see the party tomorrow night," Suzanne said to Traci. "It's going to be spectacular, our biggest turnout yet. The silent auction has some crazy stuff."

"Did your dad donate some of that wine, the Chateau Margeaux you were telling me about?" April asked.

"Yeah, he gave us a case. Someone else donated six months of their private jet membership."

Traci couldn't imagine ever needing to use a private jet, but the idea of a case of that amazing wine? That she would enjoy, but knew she could never in a million years afford it.

She was at the bottom of her second cosmo when the effects of the vodka and traveling all day caught up with her and she couldn't help yawning. Dan happened to see it and gave her hand a squeeze. "Are you ready to get out of here?"

He sent a text message quickly and then they said their good-byes and made their way downstairs and out on to the street. The same sleek car that had driven them there was waiting by the curb. Dan led her over to it and opened the door and she climbed in. Once they were settled inside and the driver started the engine, Traci turned to Dan and asked, "How did you manage this so quickly?"

"I'd given the driver a heads up earlier that we'd probably want a return ride back around this time. He told me to just text message him when we were ready and either him or another car in the area would be right over."

"Wow, that's impressive." She leaned into him and he wrapped his arm around her. It felt like just a few minutes later when Dan was gently shaking her awake and Traci realized that she'd fallen asleep within minutes of leaving the restaurant. She checked her cell phone and saw that it was nearly two in the morning. No wonder she was so tired.

She and Dan dragged themselves upstairs and then fell into bed and slept late the next morning. Traci had a slight headache. Even though she only had two drinks, she wasn't used to drinking vodka, so it didn't surprise her. She rolled over in Dan's roomy, king-sized bed and saw that she had the bed to herself. He was already up, and she heard him puttering around the kitchen and soon after, the smell of freshly brewed coffee got her out of bed, too, and she wandered into the kitchen, still half-asleep, to see what Dan was up to.

He was wide-awake and bustling around his kitchen, chopping onions and peppers and then cracking several eggs into a bowl and whipping them. Traci sat on a stool along the counter and sipped her coffee while she watched him work. He got out a saute pan, added some butter to it, then set it on the stove and turned on the heat. Once the butter melted, he added the vegetables and then a few minutes later, dumped in the eggs and used a rubber spatula to stir it all up in to a delicious smelling scrambled mixture. While it was cooking, he also threw a few pieces of bread in a toaster and then when everything was done, he split the eggs and toast between two plates and handed her one, along with a dish of butter for the toast.

"This is great," Traci said after she took her first bite.

"Thanks. Did you have fun last night?" he asked as he sat next to her and started to eat.

"I did. It was fun to meet some of your friends."

"They were dying to meet you. I've been raving."

"They were all nice. I don't have all that much in common with any of them, though. I didn't realize you moved in such a high society crowd," she teased.

Dan frowned at that. "Yeah, they can be a bit much at times. It was a little intimidating to me at first, too, but now I'm used to it."

"Guess it's just the nature of what you do," she speculated.

"I met all these guys years ago, when I first was getting going with the stock service. It's a small circle but everyone is involved with managing money in some way and following the stock market. It can be a very lucrative field."

"I gathered that."

"I kind of fell into it, you know. The original plan was to be a starving journalist. I never thought it would lead to this. I've been very lucky to find something I'm good at, and enjoy and that pays well."

"You don't have to be here to do it though, do you?"

"No. I mean it helps to be around other people in the field, but I can really do this work from anywhere, as long as there's a good internet connection. I was a little worried about that when I first got to Beauville."

"But, you were fine, right?" Traci couldn't help wishing that Dan would want to spend more time in Beauville, but that didn't seem likely. His life, and his friends, were here.

"I could come back maybe one week a month," Dan said. "That's something to consider."

"That would be wonderful."

After breakfast, they changed and Dan spent the day showing her all around Chicago, and they had lunch at one of his favorite pizza places where they were known for deep dish style pizza. Traci loved it and had never had anything like it, not even in Bozeman.

Later, as they were getting ready to head out to Suzanne's party, Traci wondered if it would be like a repeat of the prior evening but on an even more obnoxious and larger scale. She tried to think positive, but had a sinking feeling that it was going to be a long night.

Dan called ahead for the same car service they used the night before and shortly before eight, they headed out. The party was black tie, and Dan looked downright hot in his black tuxedo and Traci had bought a dress the week before that she was excited to wear. It was a flapper style cocktail dress, strapless with shiny black threads everywhere. It was simple, but very pretty and flattering and she was happy to wear the diamond tennis bracelet that Dan had given her with it.

The party was held at an art museum that had recently been renovated. There were hundreds of people already inside when they arrived and in the corner, a jazz band was playing as waiters came by with flutes of champagne and stuffed mushrooms. Traci eagerly accepted one of both and popped the mushroom in her mouth. It was a cheese and meat stuffing and was delicious. Suzanne floated over, said hello and told them to help themselves to the appetizer stations around the room. There were tables overflowing with shrimp on ice, and crab claws and more waiters coming by with crab cakes and other assorted hot items. There was also a vodka bar, with a dozen various bottles and shot glasses made out of ice to drink out of. Next to the vodka was a caviar station with bowls of caviar and all the fixings: onion, sour cream, chopped egg, and tiny pancakes and crostini to go with.

"Is there a dinner, too? I could make a meal out of all of this."

Dan chuckled, "This is just the beginning. These things usually go on for multiple courses."

He was right. After a while, they found their seats at a large round table and everyone they'd been with the night before was there. Traci had decided to stay with wine tonight, and after the initial glass of champagne that she'd enjoyed, she switched to a cabernet. The night was more enjoyable than she'd expected, largely due to the food which kept coming and Traci was careful to not eat too much so that she could enjoy whatever came next. There was a rich, sauteed foie gras first course that was served on brioche toast and had some kind of a chutney on the side. That was followed by a caesar salad and then a pasta course of spinach and sausage ravioli with proscuitto in a cream sauce that was out of this world. The main course was sliced filet mignon topped with a lobster tail and bearnaise sauce.

Once they finished dinner, Traci could barely move, she

was so full. But soon after the service ended, a new band came on and Suzanne and April were the first ones up on the dance floor. The rest of them followed and Traci was impressed to discover that Dan was actually a pretty good dancer.

The drinks kept flowing and in between dancing, they'd return to their table, where the men were drinking scotch and the girls, with the exception of Traci, were into martinis again. As it had the night before, the conversation seemed to revolve around money- who was getting it, what they were doing with it, and how they could get more of it.

"So, I liked the Range Rover that I rented out in Montana so much that I bought one, just yesterday. I love it, it looks really cute in white," Suzanne said.

"No kidding? Are you getting rid of the Mercedes then?" April asked.

"I'll never get rid of the Mercedes, she's my baby!" Suzanne laughed.

"Is it hard to keep two cars in the city?" Traci asked

Suzanne and April shot each other a glance and then Suzanne said, "No, it's a piece of cake, really. I just rented an extra spot. They're both in the garage below my building."

"Oh, that's convenient then." It had never occurred to Traci that people might actually rent parking spots. That didn't happen where she was from.

Finally, it was time for the countdown to midnight and everyone had their noisemaker ready. When the clock struck twelve, people screamed and hugged and kissed. Dan pulled Traci in and she sank into his kiss, wishing they were back in his apartment.

Almost as if he could read her mind, he said, "Do you want to go? I can use the excuse that you have an early flight."

"Yes, I just want to spend the rest of my time here with you."

They had a short wait outside for the car service and soon after were back at Dan's place where he made her feel very welcome, indeed. They crawled into his bed, but neither was tired and they stayed up for a few more hours making the most of every moment that they had left together.

The next morning, Dan insisted on going with her to the airport and they were both quiet on the cab ride over. When they got out, the cab waited a few minutes for Dan to say good-bye before driving him back home.

"It was really great having you here. I'm so glad you came."

"I'm glad I came, too. I wish you were coming back with me."

"Don't forget that I love you," Dan said as he leaned in for a final kiss good-bye.

"Me, too." Traci watched as the cab drove away and felt intense sadness wash over her. As much as she loved Dan, seeing where he lived and how he lived had opened her eyes to how very different their life-styles were. She hoped not, but she was really was afraid that they might be too different.

Chapter Twenty

Traci was in a funk all week. She spoke with Dan briefly most nights and looked forward to his calls, but was growing tired of hearing about all the different events he was attending. It seemed like he went out almost every night with his friends. It especially bothered her, for some reason, when he mentioned Suzanne. He seemed to spend an awful lot of time with her. Granted, it was usually the same group she'd met with all going out together, but Suzanne was always there and it sounded like she was usually the one making the plans. She knew it shouldn't bother her, but it did. She admitted as much to Molly when she stopped by one night after work for a glass of wine.

"Do you think she has a thing for him?" Molly asked.

"I can't say that for sure, it's just a gut sense I have. I mean, she flew across the country to visit him. Who does that?"

"Well, you did say she's a little unusual that way. Maybe it's normal behavior, for her. I mean who buys a white Range Rover because it's cute? As a second car?" Molly laughed at the idea of it.

"I know. It's just his whole crowd. I've never met anyone like them. The kind of money they talk about and throw around, it's like monopoly money. There's a never-ending supply of it."

"That must be nice."

"I don't know, but it's very different. They're just not like us."

"You'll be seeing Dan soon, though. Isn't he coming back next weekend for a visit?"

"Yeah, I can't wait to see him. I think it's that I'm missing him more than anything else. It feels so empty here."

"I know what you mean. That's what it was like when I was in Manhattan and Christian was here. Of course, we'd actually broken up then, so it was even worse. I was just going through the motions and trying to move on. But it was hard."

"Well, we're still together, sort of, so I guess that's a good thing."

"Just look on the bright side, he'll be here soon and you guys will have a blast."

Traci got home to her condo a little before eight. Dan had texted her earlier that he'd try her around nine, so that was eight her time. Sure enough, as soon as she walked in and took her shoes off, the phone rang and it was Dan. They chatted easily about their day and then Dan seemed to take a breath and said, "So, I have some good news and some bad news. Which do you want first?"

"Okay, the good news."

"Do you remember the silent auction at Suzanne's party? Well, I won something."

"You did? I don't even remember you making a bid on anything."

"I think you were out on the floor dancing. Anyway, I had the winning bid on a case of wine. The one you loved, that Suzanne brought out there, from her father's wine collection."

"You bought a case? Of that wine? Did you at least get a good deal on it? Traci knew it would be many thousands of dollars for a whole case of that wine.

Dan was quiet for a minute and then said, "Well, not exactly. At silent auctions like that for charity, you usually end up paying more than the going price. Sometimes, much more. But it's all for charity, so it's a write-off!"

Traci felt a little sick to her stomach imagining how much that must have cost him.

"That's so much money, though. I hate to have you spend so much."

"It's nothing, really. I can afford it, and like I said it's for a good cause. I thought you'd be more excited. I know how much you loved that wine."

"No, it's great, really. So, what's the bad news?"

"Well, it doesn't look like I'm going to be able to make it

back next weekend after all. I totally forgot, there's another charity thing I told Suzanne I'd go to months ago. It's kind of a big deal and lots of people are expecting me to be there."

"Oh, okay."

"But, I was thinking, why don't you come here instead? You could come with me? I'm sure Suzanne could scrape up another ticket for us."

As much as she wanted to see Dan, the thought of going to another stuffy event like that, and having to fly across the country to do so, was not at all appealing.

"Let me think about that, and get back to you."

"Oh, okay. Well, let me know soon okay? These tickets have been sold out for months, according to Suzanne."

"Right. Well, I'm disappointed that you can't make it, but I understand if you had a prior commitment. We can try for the weekend after maybe?"

"I'm sorry, babe, the next two weekends after that are booked solid. I thought I was free so said yes to a bunch of things. Right after that, though, for sure. I can't wait."

"Okay, so I'll see you a month from now, then."

"Well, hopefully next weekend, you'll come here."

Traci sighed. "I'll see." Traci heard a knock in the background and asked, "Is someone at your door?"

"It's probably Suzanne. We're heading out so I'd better run. Love you!"

"Love you, too." Traci hung up the phone and felt like crying. She was starting to think that she and Dan were not suited at all. Maybe he and Suzanne were meant to be together, she thought to herself miserably as she curled up on her sofa and pulled a soft fleece throw around her. While Dan was out gallivanting around Chicago, she was about to watch TV for a bit and then head to bed early. She wondered how anyone really managed to make a long-distance relationship work.

❦

Dan ran downstairs to catch up with Suzanne. She was waiting outside in her white Range Rover. He was surprised not to see April in the front seat. He'd thought they were all heading off to one of their favorite new restaurants.

"Where's April? I thought she was coming with us?" he said as he climbed into the front seat. Suzanne pulled the car away from the curb before he had the door completely shut. She was always in a hurry.

"She wasn't feeling well at the last minute and decided not to come. It's just the two of us tonight."

"Oh, okay. I thought Jeff and the others would be there, too?"

"They have some function with one of their clients. So, you're stuck with me, I'm afraid."

He found himself telling Suzanne a little of the conversation he'd just had with Traci.

"I really thought she'd be more excited about the wine."

"Did you tell her how much you spent on it? It cost a fortune. Most girls would be impressed by that."

"Traci's different than most girls." Dan had never met a girl who actually was concerned that he might be spending too much money. It was kind of cute in a way. He hoped that she'd decide to come to Chicago for the weekend. The main reason he was going out so much was because it was just too lonely at home if he didn't. The few nights he had stayed in, he was miserable missing Traci. As much as he enjoyed going out with his friends, because he did love to go out and socialize, he realized that his favorite nights recently had been when he was in Beauville and he and Traci would just stay in and hang out together on the sofa. Maybe he was starting to get old. He'd never been satisfied doing that before.

Suzanne pulled into the valet station outside the very exclusive-looking restaurant they were about to visit. She handed the valet her car keys and they walked in. It looked like any of the other high end restaurants he usually went to, lots of glass and steel, high ceilings, unusual menu items and a sea of suits at the bar. They made their way over to the bar and Suzanne ordered a lemon drop martini and Dan asked for a draft beer. The bartender raised his eyebrow at that, but Dan didn't care. He might be the only person drinking beer there, but it was what he wanted.

A few seats opened up at the bar and Suzanne claimed them. They sat down and surveyed the crowd. They both recognized a few familiar faces and found that by being seated, people drifted over to say hello and then drifted away as a new group of people poured in. A few hours later, they were on their third round when Suzanne surprised him by saying, "I wonder why we never dated? I mean I was off the market for a few years but still, we have so much in common. Everyone says we'd make a great couple." Her hand was suddenly resting lightly on his and Dan pulled his back and took a sip of beer. He hadn't seen this coming at all. He decided to make light of it.

"Well, if I wasn't with Traci, I'd be crazy not to go out with you. So, what did you say Jeff was doing tonight? Maybe if I text him he can meet us out here." He pulled his phone out of his pocket and started to text when Suzanne stopped him by putting her hand on the phone.

"He's out all night with clients. So, anyway, like I was saying, Traci's not here, and you're not engaged. Maybe we should see if this could work."

"Suzanne, I'm so sorry if I gave you the wrong impression, but I love Traci. I really love her."

"You do? I've never heard you say that about anyone before."

"Yeah, I do. What do you think? Do you want to head home? I'll drive this time." There was no way he was going to let Suzanne behind the wheel after three martinis and, he suspected, very little food.

"Okay. You're a good friend. Forget I said anything."

"It's forgotten."

Chapter Twenty-One

Traci ran into Billy the next day at the Morning Muffin. She'd gone there by herself and just wanted to relax a little bit before work with a cup of good coffee and one of their triple-berry scones. She was sitting by the window, sipping her coffee and keeping an eye on the time, when Billy walked in. He saw her immediately and came over.

"Are you going to be here for a few more minutes? I'd love to sit down and catch up if you have the time?"

"Sure, I have about twenty minutes or so before I have to run."

Billy went and got a coffee and a bran muffin and brought them back to the table. He looked great; he'd lost a bit of weight and had good color in his cheeks and he seemed well.

"How are you, Billy? Did everything go okay?"

"I'm good, and yeah, going there was the best thing that

could have happened to me. I'm off the pain meds completely. They worked with me on putting together a physical therapy plan that will help keep the muscles loose. And I stopped drinking. That helps, too."

"I'm so glad to hear it."

"How are you doing? Still dating Christian's brother? Is he still here?"

"Yes and no. I'm good. Still dating Dan, but he's back in Chicago now. We're doing the long-distance relationship thing."

"How's that working out for you?"

"It's hard. Really hard, sometimes. I don't love his friends, so that makes it even harder."

"You've gone there, and met them?"

Traci filled him in on what Dan's life was like in Chicago and even told him about the case of wine Dan had bought at the silent auction.

"Thousands of dollars for a case of wine? I don't get that at all."

"I know. It's delicious, but totally over-the-top."

"Are you happy?" Billy cut right to the heart of it and it was the question that she had been struggling with.

"Sometimes. When Dan was here and we were spending time together, it was just about perfect. But that was just one side of Dan. I've seen the other side now and I have to question if I fit in. If we fit together, that is."

"That's tough. I don't know what to tell you."

"I'm sorry, I must sound like such a whiner."

"You don't at all. I hope things work out for you. I really do."

"I appreciate that, Billy."

"Things are looking up for me in the love department," he said with a big smile. "You know Linda in the guidance office?" Traci had gone to school with Linda Hopkins, who worked as a guidance counselor at the high school. She was petite and blonde and a really sweet, calm person. She could see the two of them making a great match.

"Yeah, I do know Linda, she's great."

"We've gone out a few times. Seems to be going well, so far."

"I'm really happy for you, Billy." She had to go then to get to work on time and gave him a hug good-bye. She really was glad that he seemed to be turning things around.

Traci was lost in her own thoughts all day at work and when she came home she was still unclear about what she was going to say to Dan when he called. She definitely wasn't going to go to Chicago; she'd let him know that. But, she had also made another decision after seeing Billy and seeing how happy he was and in thinking about how well suited he and Linda seemed to be, it became clear that she and Dan were fooling themselves. They were not well-matched at all, and it seemed like they wanted different things. That being the case, it just didn't make sense to continue trying to make the relationship work, especially when the distance thing was so hard anyway.

She poured herself a small glass of red wine to calm her

nerves and to get her courage up. It was always difficult to end a relationship, especially when in your heart you didn't really want to let go. But in her head, she knew it was the right thing to do. Dan should find someone in Chicago, someone like Suzanne or even Suzanne herself, someone he'd be more compatible with long-term.

She jumped when the phone rang and spent the first ten minutes chatting about nothing. But then Dan asked her if she was coming out for the weekend and she couldn't put it off any longer.

"I'm not going to be able to make it out to Chicago. Honestly, I don't want to come. That kind of thing just isn't my scene, but I know you love it. I've been thinking a lot about this and as hard as it is, I think it might be best if we stop trying to make this work. I think we might be too different, in too many ways, and just don't want the same things." When she finished talking, she realized that tears were streaming down her face and she grabbed the nearest thing to her, a paper napkin, to wipe them away.

"Don't say that. We can still make this work. I love you. I miss you. Suzanne even made a pass at me this past weekend and I told her that I love you."

The only words that registered were what he said about Suzanne.

"Suzanne made a move on you?"

"Yeah, but it was nothing. I told her I love you and she understood."

"She said she understood? Dan, maybe you should be with Suzanne. She's clearly interested and she's perfect for you." Traci couldn't figure out if she was angry or just sad that what she'd suspected about Suzanne was true.

"She's not perfect for me. I'm not interested in her. Don't you hear me? I love you."

"I love you, too, but I can't do this. I'm sorry. I have to go."

Traci hung up the phone and threw herself on the sofa and cried until her nose was completely stuffed. She poured herself another glass of wine, a bigger one this time, and sat in her favorite chair, wrapped in her softest blanket, with a box of tissues by her side. She turned on the TV, and flipped the channels until she found one of her favorite movies that was about to start. It was bittersweet, though, because as much as she loved the romantic comedy classic, *When Harry Met Sally*, it totally reminded her of Dan and how they'd become such good friends before anything romantic happened. By the time the movie ended, she'd finished most of the bottle of wine and gone through an entire box of tissues. Feeling completely miserable, she finally dragged herself up and fell into bed.

Dan couldn't believe that Traci had just broken up with him. He tried her back several times but she wouldn't pick up the phone. He paced around the condo trying to figure out what to do. He was supposed to go out, Jeff was expecting him to meet him out in an hour, but that was the last thing he felt like doing. He called to cancel and told him about the call and Traci ending things.

"That's rough, man. You should go see her, maybe you can work things out. I'm here if you need me."

Dan opened a beer and hooked his iPod into his stereo receiver and turned the music up as loud as he felt his neighbors could tolerate. He walked outside and leaned over the edge of his terrace thinking about Traci, about everything. He thought again about how much his life had changed since he had broken his leg, and since he had met Traci. He thought he would hate living in Beauville and was surprised by how much he didn't hate it. He thought about how much he enjoyed teasing Mrs. O'Brien and having her fuss over him. He missed her chocolate milk shakes and her cookies. He missed hanging out with his brother and Molly. He liked that the people in Beauville were so friendly and welcoming. And he missed Traci. He missed her so much and the thought of not being with her again just felt so wrong. When they were together, everything felt right. His work was here, but as Traci had reminded him, he could do his job from anywhere. He looked around his condo. It was beautiful and he loved it, but it had never felt so empty before. He needed to get a good night's sleep and see if what he was considering doing still seemed like a good idea when he woke up.

Chapter Twenty-Two

Traci kept to herself the rest of the week. Dan had called a few more times the night she'd spoken to him, but she hadn't taken the calls and he hadn't called since. She was trying to accept that it really was over, but it was hard. Especially when Friday rolled around, and she thought about Dan going to Suzanne's big event. She was glad when Molly called and insisted that she come over for dinner and told her to bring Travis. It was always fun hanging out with them. Molly was a great cook and it would help to get her mind off Dan.

She picked up a bottle of her new favorite wine, a red zinfandel called Predator, that had a ladybug on the top of the bottle and was the second most delicious bottle of wine she'd ever had and it only cost fifteen dollars. She'd introduced Dan to it, too, recently, and he'd said it tasted every bit as good as some of the more expensive wines he'd had.

Travis was already there when she arrived, and Molly was putting some bruschetta together in the kitchen. Traci's stomach rumbled. She'd had Molly's bruschetta before and it was amazing. She said the secret was to spread a thin layer of whipped garlic and herb cheese on the warm, buttered toast before adding the topping of fresh tomatoes, garlic, olive oil, slivered basil and a hint of balsamic vinegar.

"Hi, Traci," Molly called out as she walked in. "Oh, good, you brought wine. Do you want to open it and pour us a glass?"

Traci got busy with the wine opener and then got two glasses out of the cabinet. The guys were all drinking beer. She poured them each a glass and handed one to Molly.

"Thanks," Molly said as she passed a plate of bruschetta to Traci. "These are ready. Grab one and then pass them to the guys."

Traci was on her second piece of bruschetta when she heard a car pull into the driveway and wondered if someone else was coming for dinner.

"Is someone here?" Molly asked and Christian walked over to the window.

"I don't recognize the car." He kept watching to see who it was and then turned back to everyone in surprise.

"It's Dan!" He looked at Traci then and asked, "Did you know he was coming?"

"No, he told me he wasn't going to be able to make it this weekend." She hadn't yet told any of them that they'd ended things, so her stomach suddenly churned as Dan walked in the door, carrying a case of wine.

He smiled as he set the box down on the counter. "Looks like I brought this to the right place. Something smells great."

Christian slapped him on the back and said, "Good to see you, didn't know you were coming in this weekend."

"I didn't think I was going to be able to, but I switched a few things around." He accepted a beer from Christian and then turned to Traci, "Can we go next door and talk for a minute?"

"Okay, sure." Traci felt butterflies now in her stomach as she followed Dan across the walkway to his house. He unlocked the door and they went inside.

He sat at one of the stools at his kitchen island and gestured for Traci to sit next to him.

"I thought you couldn't come this weekend?"

"I changed my mind. About a lot of things. After we hung up, I canceled my plans for the night and did a lot of thinking. Things were different for me when I got back to Chicago. I went out a lot, like I always did before, but this time it was because if I stayed home, I'd just be missing you. And you're right, my friends are great people, but they're not like us. They're focused on different things and I used to think those things were important, but I don't think they matter that much now. What matters most to me is being here, with you and with my family. I forgot what it was like to live here, and it's what I want. I thought I'd hate it, but my happiest times have been just hanging out here, with you."

"What are you saying?" Traci thought it sounded like he

was going to move back to Beauville, but she didn't want to get her hopes up.

"I'm saying that I love you." He reached deep into his pocket and pulled out a small box and opened it. A stunning, cushion cut diamond sat inside. He pulled it out and got down on his knee. "And I'm saying I want to spend the rest of my life with you, if you'll have me. Will you marry me?"

Traci was stunned. The tears started streaming down her cheeks again, but this time out of happiness.

"Of course I will."

Dan stood up,slipped the ring on her finger and then kissed her for what seemed like five minutes straight. When they came up for air, she stared at the ring again. It was lovely, and huge and much too extravagant. She couldn't stop herself from saying, "You shouldn't have gone so crazy on this. It's too much, especially after buying that wine."

Dan laughed. "Well, it's a funny thing about that wine. Let's go have a look at it and share our good news with everyone."

They walked back over and everyone must have been able to tell that something was up by the expressions on their faces. Traci held up her hand and Dan shouted, "We're engaged!"

Molly dropped her spoon and ran over to hug Traci. "I'm so happy for you!" and to Dan she said, "Congratulations!" The guys high-fived him, and Dan pulled a bottle of champagne out of a brown paper bag that he'd also carried in.

"I was hoping we'd need this," he said as Molly opened the champagne and Christian hunted around for glasses. While they were doing that, Dan told Traci to take a look inside the wine box. She thought that was an odd request as she already knew what those fancy bottles of wine looked like, but she walked over to the box anyway and looked inside. She saw twelve bottles, all with ladybugs on the top.

"You brought a case of Predator? What happened to the crazy expensive wine?"

"I sold it, used part of the money to buy your ring and put the rest in my bank account. Oh, and I kept a little out to buy a case of your second favorite wine." He was smiling at her and Traci saw so much love in his eyes that it took her breath away.

"I'm so happy that you did this, and I couldn't possibly love you any more than I do right now."

Molly passed out glasses of champagne to everyone and then Christian said a toast, "To a long and happy life together, filled with happiness and love."

They toasted, and then kissed, looking forward to spending the rest of their lives together, in Beauville.

-The End-

About the Author

Pamela Kelley lives and works in Plymouth, MA and has always been a huge book worm. She worked as a journalist many years ago and in recent years as a food writer for local papers. She is very excited to finally be following her passion to write the kinds of books she loves to read.

She also welcome emails from readers and would love to hear what you think about her books. Please feel free to email her at **pamelamkelley@gmail.com**

Made in the USA
Monee, IL
25 May 2021